SHE'S OUT

JANE BLONDE
GOLDEN SPY

JILL MARSHALL

JANE BLONDE

Goldenspy

Jill Marshall

Jill Marshall Books

First published by Macmillan Children's Books 2008

Copyright © Jill Marshall

A CIP catalogue record for this book is available from the National Library of New Zealand

ISBN 978-1-99-002425-2 Paperback

Cover Design by Katie Gannon

Illustrations by Madison Fotti-Knowles

Prologue

It had taken all his strength, every ounce of his extraordinary intelligence, to extract himself from the Earth. Now he had to be free of it – forever. Free from the cloying cold that numbed his thoughts and his movements. Free from the pitiful, powerless race who dared, somehow, to condemn him. And free, by whatever means it took, from the SPIs who tried at every turn to stop him, irritating him like mosquitoes, thwarting even his most brilliant manoeuvres.

As for Jane Blonde . . . the mere thought of her made his internal organs cramp with bitter rage. She was the most aggravating of all. Even more so than her conceited, know-it-all father. But she wouldn't stop him this time. All the Jane Blondes in the world would not be enough to spoil this plan. He had full control, right at his fingertips – or the tips of his tentacles, since Blonde had turned him into this mutant monster. – No matter. He laughed quietly, the full beam of his gaze taking in the scene before him, the scene he would soon destroy. It was only a matter of time now. Just a matter of time . . .

Chapter 1 Zoo's news

The last week of the school year had come around amazingly quickly. And it wasn't just the speed at which it had passed that had been amazing, thought Janey Brown as she waited in the queue for the coach, pulling her hat down further to stop the sun burning her nose. The year had quite simply been out-of-this-world.

'Don't sit at the back,' said her best friend, Alfie, giving her a shove. 'Those goons will just want to wave at people out the back window. And not there either,' he added, shuddering as he saw which seat Janey had been about to plonk herself into. 'Too near Mum.'

'Your mum's coming?' Janey was surprised. Alfie's mum was the headmistress of Winton School, but as she didn't have a class of her own she didn't normally go on school trips with the pupils.

'Are you kidding?' Alfie plonked himself down next to Janey. 'Her two favourite pupils are going – that's you and me, in case you hadn't realised – on our last ever school trip from Winton. And where are we going?'

'Solfari Lands,' said Janey with a grin.

No wonder Mrs Halliday couldn't resist. Solfari Lands was the wildlife park operated by Janey's own father, Boz Brilliance Brown, Superspy, master of disguise, and head of his own spying organisation, Solomon's PolifICAtional Investigations – or SPI. His team included Mrs Halliday and Alfie, otherwise known as Agent Halo and Spylet Al

Halo; Janey's exuberant SPI Kid Educator – or SPI:KE – who went by the name of G-Mamma, and various other spies and spylets, with Jane Blonde, Sensational Spylet proving to be the greatest of them all.

Janey still found it hard to believe that when she stepped into the Wower, the super-charged spy shower in G-Mamma's Spylab, as an ordinary, mousey-haired school-girl, she emerged as her platinum blonde, multi-gadgeted alter-ego, Jane Blonde. But it was true. And that was what had made the year so completely incredible – along with the various gadgets she'd employed, the friendships she'd established, and the death-defying missions she'd been hurled on to protect her father, her fellow SPIs and spylets, and even the Earth itself, from destruction at the hands of the mad scientific genius – rogue spy – Copernicus. Who also happened to be Alfie's father.

Mrs Halliday clambered up the coach steps and clapped her hands. 'Well, boys and girls, here we are… Your very last trip, before you all go your separate ways after the summer holidays. Let's make the most of it. And Jake Bell,' she said loudly to one of the 'goons' on the back seat, 'if you even think of sticking your tongue out through that back window, I'll make you stay with me at Winton for another year.'

Nothing gets passed Agent Halo! thought Janey.

She smiled at her head-teacher as she walked by, counting heads. Mrs Halliday's hand paused over Janey's hair, and then she dropped her hand in a sudden, furtive flick, and moved on down the bus. Janey looked down to find a note in her lap.

She opened it eagerly and read it to Alfie in a whisper. 'Lunch for you and A with your father. 12.30. Usual place. I'll cover.' Mrs Halliday had signed off with a flat oval-shape – a halo.

Janey was so excited she nearly jumped out of her seat. Instead she settled for grabbing her friend by the elbow. 'Alfie! My dad's here!'

'So it seems,' said Alfie d. 'Wonder who he'll be this time?'

'Hmmmm. Good question.' Over the course of the missions that Janey had completed, her father had turned up either as himself (dark-haired, blue-eyed Boz Brown), or as the version of himself he'd created by going through the dangerous Crystal Clarification process – tall, sandy-haired, brown-eyed Abe Rownigan. And he had another alter ego – Solomon Brown. Janey gave herself a little squeeze. She didn't care which body he turned up in. It was just enough that he was going to be there.

The sun beat down on the coach windows as they meandered their way further into the surrounding countryside. *The usual place*, thought Janey, fanning herself absently with the note from Mrs Halliday. She must mean the Spylab hidden away beneath the Amphibian House, under the holographic North American Wood Frogs that had inspired her father's first experiments. Only true

SPI members would know its location, and Janey could hardly stop herself from running straight there as the coach pulled up in the car park.

'Steady,' said Alfie, seeing how excited she was. 'It's only eleven o'clock.'

'I know,' moaned Janey. 'It's so frustrating. Imagine having your dad so close and not being able to see him … oh. Sorry.'

Alfie shrugged at the mention of his father. Last time he'd seen him, Copernicus had been SatiSPIed, SPInamited, and Wowed by Jane Blonde, pretty much all at the same time – and the results had not been pretty. Alfie's evil father was now a revolting squid-like creature, who the SPI team had sent to his death in the depths of the earth. 'Not seeing my father is a very good thing, believe me.'

'Oh look,' said Janey, changing the subject. 'Monkeys! Aren't they cute?'

The class stood back and watched cages were unloaded from the back of a gigantic truck. There were tiny marmosets and lemurs, black, furry chimpanzees and two vast crates, each containing a bored-looking, marmalade-coloured Orang Utang. 'Don't touch,' warned one of the men as the class gathered around it. 'Some of these can give you nasty bites.'

Janey looked at the nearest chimp. He was cuddled up against a slightly bigger chimpanzee, and didn't look capable of hurting a fly, let alone a person. Her heart went out to him, and unthinkingly, she gave him a tiny wave. 'Hello, little chimp.'

The chimp looked back at her with shiny round eyes, and suddenly moved his hand around in a circle. Janey gasped. 'He waved at me!' She grabbed Alfie's arm and pointed at the cage. 'That one! I waved at him and he did a … a circle thing back at me.'

'A circle thing?' Alfie looked closely at the two chimpanzees. 'I think he was just lifting his … what is it, a hand or paw? Anyway, look, he was just picking out the other one's fleas. That's disgusting,' he said loudly to the chimp, who blinked at him solemnly and then carried on combing through the other's coat.

'You're probably right,' said Janey, a little disappointed. 'Let's go and look at the rhinos.'

They wandered around the wildlife park ambling in the sunshine in a great loop that took them past hippos, rhinoceros and tigers, enclosures of deer, impala, and zebra, then down a hill into the tropical bird aviary. The next stop was the Amphibian House. Janey checked her watch. 12.20. Not long now before she could see her dad.

Sure enough, Mrs Halliday shot her a quick, knowing glance before calling all the children to her. 'It's about time we had some lunch. The picnic area's just behind those trees. She stood like a traffic warden, arms out, waving the class through the gap in the trees until Janey and Alfie were the only ones left. 'Back here in forty-five minutes,' she muttered out of the side of her mouth, before marching through the grass towards the picnic area.

As Janey pushed through the doors of the Amphibian House, her heart began to thud with anticipation. Last time she had been here, she'd been trapped in the Spylab by the evil Sinerlesse leader, Ariel. Janey was now ten time the spylet she had been on her first mission. She pressed the red eye of a model tree-frog, and stepped onto the cushion of air at the top of the entry tube that led down into her father's Spylab.

Janey and Alfie scrambled to their knees in the stark light of the lab, and looked around for her father. 'There you are,' said a deep voice, and suddenly Janey was wrapped in a warm hug, her nose pressed into a salmon-pink Solfari Lands polo shirt.

Her father held her at arm's length, and Janey looked up at the crinkly brown eyes and flashing grin of Abe Rownigan. 'You look well,' he said gently.

'So do you,' said Janey, her smile so big that her eyes had become slits, and she could hardly see.

Abe reached over and shook Alfie's hand. 'Al, good to see you.'

'You too. Thanks for inviting me for lunch,' said Alfie. 'Sir,' he added as an afterthought, going slightly pink.

'Ah, yes. Lunch.' Abe looked around the laboratory, rubbing his hands through his hair so it stood up in curls. 'I

7

forgot about that. I could check the fridge. G-Mamma might have filled it up last time she was here.'

'It doesn't matter. We've got our sandwiches with us.' Janey jostled her back-pack around so he could see, and Abe smiled.

'Great. Sandwiches it is. You eat,' he said, leading them to one of the workbenches, 'and I'll talk.'

Janey knew that her father put himself in danger whenever he came out of hiding. He must have something very important to share with her and Alfie. The atmosphere was electric, and Abe was pacing around the bench. What was on his mind?

'Sandwich?' Janey offered.

'Did your mum make them?' Abe grinned. Jean Brown's lack of kitchen skills was legendary in their family. Of course, she had other legendary skills, namely the ones she'd used as super-SPI, Gina Bellarina, before she'd been brain-wiped.

'I made them,' Janey said with a grin.

Abe shook his head anyway. 'I'm too fired up to eat, to be honest.'

'Has something happened, sir?' Alfie opened his lunchbox and fiddled anxiously with a sausage roll. 'You don't think that my da—''No,' said Abe looking directly at Alfie 'There's no evidence that Copernicus has resurfaced. But I'm going to need your help guarding the Spylab.'

Janey and Alfie both sat forward eagerly. Something WAS afoot, and that meant one thing – a new mission.

Abe paused, staring at his feet as though the enormity of this mission weighed him down. 'I've discovered something. Something enormous. A … process, I suppose you'd call it.'

'Like Crystal Clarification?' said Janey breathlessly. Her blood was racing through her veins, nervous excitement mounting with every word.

Her father nodded. 'Yes. But bigger. Bigger than Crystal Clarification, and the Nine Lives theory, and the cloning process.' He ticked off the scientific discoveries on his fingers. 'This is … extreme. It could affect the whole of mankind.'

Janey held her breath, eyes shining. Alfie gasped, his sausage roll halfway to his wide-open mouth and his eyes round with anticipation.

Abe leaned in closely. 'This has to remain top secret. It's a revolution.'

Janey's gaze faltered for a moment. The only revolutions she'd ever heard of had involved guns and battles. 'You're starting a war?'

'No, no,' said her father quickly. 'That's the name of the new process I've discovered.'

'Revolution,' whispered Janey.

She exchanged glances with Janey. Even without saying anything more, they both knew the truth.

This mission was going to be their biggest yet.

Chapter 2 Crazy days

The second Janey got home, she made an excuse to her mum and charged up the stairs to her bedroom. She closed the door behind her, and made straight for the fireplace. As soon as she pressed wall at the ten-past-two position, the panel at the back of the hearth slid upwards, and Janey dropped to her hands and knees and crawled, army-style, through the opening. Going through this secret passage to G-Mamma's Spylab next door was now second nature to Janey.

She found G-Mamma busy at work, painting a portrait of Trouble. He'd clearly been through the Wower. His eyes gleamed like bright emeralds, go-faster stripes glistened along each side of his body, and his tail bristled thick and glossy. G-Mamma had also draped a yellow feather boa around his neck and garbed him in a neat leather waistcoat. They both looked up as Janey entered the Spylab, Trouble looking rather pleased with himself, and G-Mamma daubed in a rainbow of paint. 'Whaddya think, Zany Janey?' she said, spinning the portrait around.

It was surprisingly good in a completely crazy kind of a way, and Janey had to stifle a laugh. 'It's… er… great. But listen. You'll never guess what happened at Solfari Lands.'

'Well, let me try. Your father turned up and told you about a meeting at midnight tonight, with some of the other spies and spylets.' G-Mamma pointed to the pineapple-sized SPI Visualator around her neck. 'Agent Halo filled me in.'

'It's so exciting!' said Janey. 'He's made a new discovery and it's enormous and we're going to have to patrol Solfari Lands and guard his secret lab!.'

G-Mamma looked down at her lilac ball-gown and huge, specially-made glass slippers. 'Your father had better not make us wear that revolting uniform. A polo-shirt? In *prawn*-pink? Not for me, no sireee!'

Janey rolled her eyes but patted her SPI:KE's arm soothingly. 'Don't worry. We'll be in our spy gear. I'll come back to Wow up later.'

'Right you are, Blondette,' said G-Mamma, checking the clock. 'We'll re-con in seven hours. You dad's improved the SATISPY system so we'll zap ourselves. Now, go and do your daughterly duties and keep Mumsy out of the way.' She pointed to the screen projected onto the massive fridge: next door, Jean Brown was heading up the stairs.

Janey dived for the fireplace tunnel, and just managed to get onto her own hearth as her mother entered the room with a pile of clothes. 'Put these away, please, and then we'll …'

Jean Brown stopped suddenly and ducked her head, staring directly behind Janey into the fireplace. Janey winced. She hadn't had time to close the panel between her room and the Spylab; any minute now her mum would discover what she was up to every night. They'd move house. Her spy life would be over …

'What is …' Her mum glared at her. 'How did you get *paint* in your fireplace?'

Janey spun around. Magenta paint was snaking its way across the hearth, but to her great relief, the passageway was closed off. G-Mamma must have activated the panel for her, spilling a pot of paint in the process. Smiling regretfully, she said, 'Sorry, Mum. I … there was a spider in there and I threw the nearest thing at it.'

Jean raised an eyebrow. 'Hmmm. Well, make sure you clear it up.' She then dropped the laundry stack onto the end of Janey's bed and sat down next to it. 'Just one more day before the summer holidays, and we haven't organized a thing. Shall we book a holiday?' She beamed at Janey, who wondered once more how she was going to let her mum down without hurting her feelings.

'Oh, I don't know… the weather's nice here. We could just hang around at home, couldn't we?' At home, near Solfari lands, available for spy-work . .   .They couldn't go away *now*.

Jean looked a little disappointed, then shrugged. 'All right. I've got some time off work. Joy's going to stand in for me. Why don't we do a few day trips?'

Janey nodded, and gave her mum a hug. 'Day trips sound perfect. The one to the Wildlife park today was fantastic.'

'Okay. Think of some places you'd like to go,' said Jean Brown, getting up from the bed. 'And tea's ready in half an hour.'

It was really impossible to fathom, thought Janey over her sausage, chips, and baked beans, how Jean Brown could be so ignorant of Janey's other life, particularly when she herself had once been a Super-SPI. Janey realised how good she had become at acting, playing a role. Or lying, as her mother might call it.

But any guilt Janey felt about hiding her double life was soothed away a few hours later as the Wower's robotic arms massaged her bony shoulders, encased her in silver lycra and kitted her out in Fleet-feet, Girl-Gauntlet and slender black Ultra-gogs. She felt only a surge of excitement and power as a mirage of swirling droplets spun her hair into a platinum ponytail, and a cool female voice informed her, . 'Jane Blonde, Sensational Spylet: you are ready for action.' .

G-Mamma was already Wowed, a vision in striped fuchsia and a veiled turban which made her look rather like a fancy marquee. 'That's better,' she said approvingly, looking Janey up and down. 'I'm rather fond of Jane the Blonde.'

Janey sensed a rap coming on, so she scooped up Trouble and set him down under the sky-light. She then entered the coordinates for Solfari Lands and pressed the SATISPY remote. The spy cat disintegrated before their eyes and shot up through the skylight in tiny pieces, like bubbles in a bottle of pop.

'You next,' said G-Mamma, taking the remote.

Janey stationed herself where Trouble had been standing, and waited for the peculiar pins-and-needles sensation as her cells split away from each other and then zinged up to a satellite in space. As ever, a wave of nausea hit as she neared the satellite, then she was streaming back down to Earth in a river of cells, which joined together so her body reconnected before her eyes, and the floor of the Solfari Lands spy-lab loomed up at her.

They were among the last to arrive. Other SPIs and spylets were leaning against the workbenches, chatting quietly as G-Mamma plummeted through the sky-light, which, by day, just looked like a square of turf.

Janey looked around. Alfie and his mum were there, of course, and several other families of SPIs she'd already met: Titian Ambition, known as Tish, and her mother Magenta in their trademark red spy-suits; Leaf Erikssen, in racing green along with his father Ivan, and Eagle and Peregrine with their spylet twins, Rook and . . .

Blackbird? Janey did a double-take. Blackbird had disappeared on their last mission, and was almost certainly responsible for feeding information to Copernicus! Tish was also glaring at the spylet in the shimmering, feather-covered black Spysuit. Janey almost grinned in spite of her shock: Tish could never keep her feelings to herself.

'Welcome, everyone,' said Abe, stepping through a door at the back of the lab. 'G-Mamma, could you close off the sky-light?'

G-Mamma pushed a button under the little window and the square of earth dropped back into place.

'Thank you. You'll all need to make sure it's the first thing you do when you arrive for patrol.'

'Patrol?' said Leaf, his Scandinavian accent as delicate as his appearance. 'Like in the army?'

'If you like.' Abe pointed to the door he had just come through. 'Let me explain myself more clearly. That room is the location of my most amazing – and frightening – discovery so far. It's a process I'm calling Revolution. I'm sorry that I can't tell you any more about it. I think the less you know, the better it will be if you are captured.'

'And … like, tortured?' said Alfie quietly.

Abe sighed. 'I sincerely hope it never comes to that, but there is always the danger that our enemies will find out about it and try to pressure you into telling them what you know. So I won't be letting you into that room, for your own safety. However, for *my* safety and the protection of the Revolution secret, I want a guard around the Spylab, twenty-four-seven. It's not your most exciting mission, I'm afraid. But it could be your most vital.'

Everyone was quiet as they wondered what miraculous discovery Abe had made. Suddenly a peculiar chattering noise cut through the silence. *That came from behind that door*, thought Janey. *There must be another* *room through there…*She looked at her father, her eyebrows raised.

Abe cleared her throat. 'No one is to go through the door,' he said with cool finally, pausing after every word. 'Now, Halo, can I leave the organization of this mission to you?'

'Of course,' said Mrs Halliday. 'I'll draw up a rota . School timetables, you know – I'm pretty good at that kind of thing.'

For the first time since they had arrived, Abe's face relaxed into a genuine film-star grin. 'Perfect. We'll start tonight, if that's okay. Everyone to take their times from Halo.'

'Me first, Maisie!' yelled G-Mamma, swirling her hips like a deep pink tornado. 'Blonde and I will do the first stint. If you like …' she added, as Magenta and Ivan frowned in her direction.

Mrs Halliday nodded. 'That's fine. There are twelve of us, so we can have four spies each on three eight-hour shifts. Blonde, Al Halo, G-Mamma and I will take this 10pm – 6 am shift, so Blonde's back home before her mother suspects anything. Then Leaf and Ivan, Tish and Magenta – are you okay for six until two pm? And then the Bird family, you'll be two till ten. We'll rotate after a week.'

Janey looked around at the people in the room. Her father was watching everyone's reactions with great interest, and he wasn't the only one. Blackbird's dark gaze

16

flicked anxiously from one person to the next. Janey had to say something.

She raised her hand slowly. 'Um, I don't want to be mean, we all know there's a double agent in the room.' Nobody said anything, although Blackbird's head dropped instantly. 'Blackbird, you gave my ESPIdrills to Copernicus, so that he could find out the exact formation of the centre of the earth. Why should I trust you?'

To her surprise, Blackbird burst into tears. 'I didn't know what he wanted them for. I nearly caused the whole Earth to be destroyed.'

'But why?' said Janey gently.

Blackbird sniffed noisily and shook her head, looking more bird-like than ever. 'I was stupid, that's why. I was just trying to be important, like all the rest of you were. I wasn't picked for the mission, and I wasn't very good at anything, and ...'

'I was not picked for the mission, either,' said Leaf bitterly. 'But did I go become a traitor? No. I, Leaf Erikssen, directly descended from the man who first discovered America, was not chosen, and still I acted with respect. Why could you not do that?'

'You're descended from Columbus?' said Alfie, incredulously. 'Wasn't he Spanish or something?'

'No, no, no. From Leif Erikssen, the Viking,' Leaf snapped as he turned back to Blackbird. 'So?'

'Co...Copernicus said I could be his chief spylet if I just got him your ESPIdrills. I'm ...so sorry.' And she burst into racking sobs. Rook, who up until then had been looking rather disgusted, patted his sister awkwardly on the back.

Abe held up a hand. 'Look, I knew this would be a concern for you, but I have spoken to Blackbird, and I am quite confident that she made an error of judgement. And that she is now completely loyal to our cause.'

'It am! It really, really am,' wailed Blackbird, wiping her nose on her feathery arm.

'So can we all agree to forget about that incident?' Abe looked at each of his SPIs and spylets in turn, Leaf first, and they all stared intently at Blackbird and then nodded slowly.

Janey suddenly felt sorry for Blackbird. She'd made a few wrong decisions herself in the past, guided by her emotions rather than by logic. She'd even been tempted to give up spying altogether, simply because hadn't been chosen for the last mission either. And if her dad trusted the other spylet ... She smiled at Blackbird. 'Okay,' she said softly. 'All forgotten.'

And so the first patrol settled in for the evening, and the mission – to protect Revolution – began.

As soon as Janey got into school the next morning, she was called to Mrs Halliday's office. Alfie was present, and he shrugged, mystified, as Janey walked in.

'We're needed back at the Solfari Lands lab,' said Mrs Halliday briefly. 'We'll have to go as soon as school finishes. Thank goodness it's a half-day today.'

'What's happened?' Janey thought instantly of her father. 'Is Dad okay?'

'He's fine, but he's not very happy,' said Mrs Halliday. 'During the handover between our shift and the next, something went missing - something vital to Revolution.'

'Well, we haven't got it,' said Alfie indignantly. 'Whatever *it* is,' he added hastily.

Mrs Halliday looked grim but would say no more. Janey was bursting with questions and worries but had to contain herself for the rest of the morning. What was the mysterious stolen object ? Were they under suspicion? Whatever had disappeared *had* gone missing just as their shift was going home. Now, surely her father wouldn't suspect *them*? Would he?

Chapter 3 Monkey mayhem

someone stole a monkey?' Janey gazed at her father, perplexed. 'How would they steal a monkey? And, um, why?!' But then Janey remembered the noise they had heard last night . . .the noise that had come from her father's Revolution room. A monkey . . .

'When did you notice it was gone?' said Alfie sensibly.

'Eight o'clock this morning,' said Abe

'Aha!' Alfie jumped to his feet and paced the room, a mini Sherlock Holmes in school uniform. 'So it could have disappeared at any time during the night. It could have been on either shift, or even before we'd all gathered here at midnight.'

Abe nodded. 'You're right. Which means someone may well know about Revolution . . .' Janey had never seen her father look so grave.

'You know what does seem weird though,' said Janey suddenly. 'The one person we have most reason to be worried about wasn't on either of those shifts. Maybe Blackbird arranged it especially so that all the suspicion would fall on us.'

The others looked at her, one or two of them starting to nod their agreement, 'That is right,' said Leaf. 'She has set us up.'

'It doesn't make sense,' said Abe shortly. 'Blackbird is desperate to be one of us again. She'd know she'd be the first one to fall under the spotlight.'

'And anyway, old Copper Knickers is dead,' said G-Mamma. 'There's nobody to pull her strings.'

That was true. They all looked glumly at each other, unable to come up with any solutions or sensible suggestions. Then Janey said the most horrible thing of all. 'Maybe he's not.'

'Maybe who's not what, Jane the Insanc?' G Mamma's bright blue eye peered at her through the hole of a doughnut, purchased from the Solfari Lands Café as they arrived.   Janey swallowed slowly. 'Maybe Copernicus isn't dead. I know he should be, buried deep down in the Antarctic in a broken rocket, but SPUD Nik managed to get out …' Her robot penguin had been trapped with Copernicus, but he'd escaped.

'No,' said Alfie, almost spitting out the word. 'Not again. He was meant to be dead after you Spynamited him in the Wower.'

'And he wasn't.' Janey looked around at the solemn faces. 'I think he's free. Somehow.'

Her father had already turned to the computer and as G-Mamma slammed a fist into her other hand. 'Oh, you just lemme at him,' she growled. I'll squish that squid, righty almighty. Like this!' She leapt out of her seat and mimed the actions to her rap:

'I'll squish him, uhuh uhuh,

21

I'll squish him dead ….

By sitting, uhuh uhuh,

On his squiddy head.'

She looked so ferocious that no one dared laugh. Then Abe looked up from the computer. His face was ashen.

'It's not good news,' he said.

He swivelled the computer screen round to show them the article he'd found on an international news website. 'Mutant Squid sighted in warm waters,' ran the headline:

Holiday makers surfing off the Florida coast near Titusville were staggered to find an unusual creature sharing the sea with them. Several eye-witnesses have sworn that they barely avoided being wrapped up in the tentacles of a strange octopus-like creature. Said Michael Palfreyman from the University of West Florida: 'It really sounds like a Colossal Squid, which is pretty amazing: most other sightings have been in the dark, freezing waters of the Antarctic, like the vast specimen picked up by fishermen near New Zealand recently.' The creature is thought to have been damaged in a fight, perhaps with a shark, as one eye is barely visible while the other is huge and yellow. Coast guards are warning swimmers and surfers to be vigilant.

Janey's worst fear had just been realised. Copernicus was back. 'That's got to be him,' she said. 'Usually seen in the Antarctic, one eye bigger than the other...'

'But what's he doing in *Florida*?' asked Tish.

Alfie opened a new packet of chewing gum and started chomping furiously. 'Maybe he's having a holiday,' he said hopefully. 'Must be tiring, after all, when you keep …' he chewed a bit harder, '…escaping…' and he worried the gum between his front teeth, '… DEATH.'

But Janey knew – they all knew – that the truth had to be more sinister. Wherever Copernicus was, there was danger. And wherever danger was, thought Janey, someone else should be.

Jane Blonde.

'I have to go to Florida,' she said decisively.

Abe stared at her for a moment, seeming to struggle between his wish to keep her safe as his daughter, and his need to get his best spies on the job to tackle his arch-enemy. He was thinking out loud. 'He's luring us to him . . . he's recruited someone to steal from me while he's busy preparing to wreak havoc in America. Now it's like he's calling us . . .I can't let you go . . .But we need to know exactly how far he's got with Revolution . . . .' Then he suddenly nodded. 'Yes. Janey, I need you to go. But not on your own.'

Alfie let out a low growl which startled everyone. 'I'll go too.' He glared at Leaf who'd dared to look at him. 'My father. My problem.'

'All right, Alfie,' said his mother. 'But I'm coming as well.'

'And me!' yelped G-Mamma.

The others all looked to volunteer, so Abe tapped on the table to get everyone's attention. 'I do still need some of you here,' he said with a rueful smile. 'G-Mamma, if you and Leaf could take over the night shift, I'd be very grateful. Magenta and Tish, the early shift. And Ivan, I'm going to need your cell-tracing expertise in this new process, if that's all right with you?'

The SPIs and spylets agreed readily, although G-Mamma and Leaf still looked a tiny bit mutinous. Both hated to be left out of the most exciting – and dangerous – part of the mission.

'We'll catch whoever's monkey-stealing,' G-Mamma muttered in a loud aside to Leaf, determined to make their work matter every bit as much as the Florida trio. 'I'll get Agent Dubbo Seven over from Oz – he's good at tracking and what have you. We'll track 'em and sack 'em.'

'Track them and sack them,' agreed Leaf earnestly.

So, with the arrangements in place, they all headed off to their various home locations to prepare for the next part of their mission. As they pulled up near her house, Mrs Halliday eyed Janey in the mirror. 'So how do we deal with your mum this time, Janey?'

Janey groaned. Her mum. Six weeks' holiday ahead of them, time off work, day trips planned, and now Janey was going to disappear.

And suddenly she decided. This time, it was going to be different.

'Just leave Mum to me,' she said with a smile. 'But send us an email to let me know where we're staying.'

Still grinning, Janey ran in the house. She threw her arms around her mum and gave her a big squeeze.

'You must have had a good last day,' said her mother breathlessly.

'I did,' said Janey, although she wasn't about to reveal why. 'And I've changed my mind. Let's go on holiday.'

'Really?' said Jean, pleased and very excited.

Janey nodded. 'I'd really love to go to Florida. Tonight!'

'Well, we don't need to …' Jean Brown stopped, and then threw her hands in the air. 'Oh, why not? I'm sure I can get something on the internet.'

Strangely enough, the Hallidays had decided to do exactly the same thing, and had emailed suggesting two side-by-side villas, next to a pool, and close to all the main attractions. They'd even managed to get four seats on a very small plane leaving that very evening. Oh, and Mrs Halliday was happy to book the whole thing on her credit card, and Janey's mum could just pay her back. Sometimes, thought Janey, having a dad who was head of a spying organisation definitely had its perks. As her slightly-bewildered mum started to pack, Janey ran upstairs to tell G-Mamma.

'Okay,' said G-Mamma sniffily. 'But don't you go getting sunstroke, and do not have too much of a good time without me.'

Janey laughed. 'I'm going on a mission remember, not a *holiday*.'

'Hmph. Well, choppity-chop, we'd better get you ready,' said G-Mamma.

The Wower door hissed closed behind Janey.

'Wow me,' she said firmly. Then she closed her eyes dreamily as the magical, transformational mist descended around her.

When she stepped out a few minutes later, G-Mamma squinted at her and then stumbled around the lab, screaming, 'My eyes, my cherry-pie eyes, I'm blinded!' She stopped abruptly. 'You look like an Oscar statuette. Blondette, the Oscarette!'

'What are you talking about?'

But then Janey turned to look at herself in the long-mirrored door of the Wower– and clapped a hand over her mouth. G-Mamma was right! Janey's silver Jane Blonde outfit had been exchanged for a gleaming golden SPIsuit, like the wetsuits she had seen surfers wear. In place of her Ultra-gogs was a pair of large coppery sunglasses, with little diamante trims along the frame. On were summery flip-flops, golden to match her SPIsuit, and her ponytail, sleek and platinum blonde, peeked out of a very cool, khaki-coloured cap.

'What happened?' she asked, stunned.

G-Mamma rifled around in a cupboard as she explained: 'Golden Spysuit. Perfect for the summer! And I guess it was time you had an upgrade! Now, your sunglasses function just like your Ultra-gogs, apart from the diamond glass-cutter studs in the frames. Might be useful – you never know. Groovy cap – that's a PERSPIRE: a Personal SPI Remote Educator, or a tiny computer to you. And finally, those flip-flops. New Fleet-Feet design – we're calling them Flip-Flop-Fleet-Feet. Four-Fs for short. Just as fast, just as springy, but the left one works like a circular saw if you whizz it along on its side. Oh, and the right doubles as a Frisbee. Perfect for the beach.'

Janey couldn't stop staring at her reflection, and then she started to giggle. If her outfit was this over-the-top, what was Alfie's going to be like?

Suddenly G-Mamma stopped rummaging. 'You'll be needing this. A surf-board sized Aeronautical SPI Conveyor!'

'Wow,' was just about all that Janey could manage.

And anyway, it was time to go. Pushing the surfboard ASPIC through the fireplace passage, Janey turned and gave G-Mamma a quick hug.

'Send me a postcard,' said her SPI:KE in a small voice, two of her several chins wobbling dangerously. 'And don't' worry, I'll take good care of Trouble.'

'Thanks, G-Mamma. I'll contact you on the SPIV. Bye, Twubs! I'll miss you!'

An hour and a half later, as her mum, Mrs Halliday, Alfie in blue silky board shorts, rash shirt and Four-Fs, and Janey with a skirt and tee-shirt over the golden glamour of her spy outfit, climbed the steps to the plane. We look exactly like what Mum thinks we are: tourists, on holiday. As if, thought Janey..

Chapter 4 Villa del sol

The holiday villas were in a tiny complex in Orlando – just four tall terraces, around a sparkling kidney-shaped pool, each painted a different ice-cream shade: vanilla, strawberry, pistachio and coffee l. Jean Brown's eyes widened as the chauffeured car pulled through the great iron gates.

'Villa del Sol,' she read aloud as they passed the sign. 'Villa of the sun, I suppose. Nice. Maisie, you really did get an amazing deal with this place.'

Janey knew that 'Sol' had more to do with Solomon Brown, one of her father's identities, but she just smiled sweetly at her mum and waited for the car to stop. It was dark, almost midnight still in Florida despite the fact that they had just flown for ten hours through the night, but the chauffeur seemed more than happy to lug their suitcases and surfboards to their respective holiday homes, and flick on the lights for them. 'Thank you,' said Jean, self-consciously holding out a few dollars for a tip.

The chauffeur waved it away. 'No problem. Courtesy of Villa Del Sol, ma'am. Now make sure you use that air-conditioning – it's so hot during the day it's a wonder the pool doesn't bubble.'

'Erm, thank you,' said Jean again, and the chauffeur tipped his hat at Janey and set off in the car again.

'I'll just go and see what the Hallidays' villa is like,' she said, after a quick glance around the tiled ground floor with its little kitchenette and cane lounge furniture. Jean was already fiddling with the control for the air-con, so Janey slipped next door.

Alfie was sprawled across the large cane sofa as Mrs Halliday bustled around the kitchenette, making tea. 'Your father thought of everything, Janey,' she said after checking that Mrs Brown wasn't behind her. 'Lady Grey tea, my favourite.'

'So where's the Spylab?' Janey didn't want to waste any time. As soon as her mum was asleep they could set off in search of Copernicus.

'Give us a break, we only just got here!' Alfie slipped off the sofa onto the tiles. 'Oooo, cooler down here.'

Mrs Halliday rattled some cups and saucers. 'I think Alfie's right for once, Janey. We should gather our strength for tonight, and make sure your mum's all settled in so she doesn't suspect anyth...oh! There you are, Jean. Cup of tea?'

Jean looked from one to the other of them. 'So she doesn't suspect what?'

She'd heard. Janey forced her jet-lagged brain to think of something, and quickly. 'Erm, Mrs Halliday just admitted that she knows the person who owns these villas, so we've got them really cheap.'

'Oh, but we can pay full price ...' As Jean reacted in exactly the way Janey had known she would, the crisis was averted.

'If we don't have to, why should we?' Mrs Halliday passed Janey a cup of tea with a grateful look. 'They weren't booked for these two weeks, so we're doing them a favour, really.'

Janey's mum seemed satisfied with this, and after a few slurps at her tea, she put the cup down. 'I know I've just sat down for ten hours straight, but I'm suddenly exhausted. And it is midnight, our time, after all. Janey, you and I are off to bed.'

'And so are we.' Mrs Halliday stifled a yawn. 'Then we can make the most of tomorrow.'

'Yeah. Can't wait to see Mickey Mouse,' said Alfie.

'Aww,' said Janey.

'I was joking. Du-uh.'

Laughing, Janey and her mum trotted back to their temporary pale-green home. She was actually very tired, Janey realised. With no Wower to revive her and keep her alert, sleep was upon her as soon as her head hit the cool linen pillow …

The sun streaming through the wooden blinds woke her after what seemed like only seconds. She could hear her mum having a shower, singing to herself, so Janey ambled downstairs and had a good look at their surroundings. There were no fireplaces, no cellars, and no unexplained cupboards, so there was no obvious location for the Spy-lab, but Janey was pretty convinced there must be one around. It was already warm, so she stripped off the pajamas that covered her golden Spysuit and lifted her face and arms to the sun.

'And Janey Brown steps up to take her dive...' said a sarcastic voice somewhere above her head.

Alfie was leaning out of his bedroom window. 'Come down,' Janey said to him. 'It's really gorgeous.'

'We've got work to do, remember? Your dad sent this through,' he added in a hiss, dropping a piece of paper to the ground.

'As if I'd forget.' Janey stuck her tongue out at him as she scooped up the note, quickly turning it into a grin for her mother as Jean appeared in the doorway.

'Morning, darling,' said Jean, in a happy sin-song voice. 'Alfie, I thought we could all have breakfast together and work out what to do today. Ask your mum for me, will you?'

Alfie withdrew his head from the window and Jean put her arms around her daughter. 'Isn't this lovely? What a fabulous idea. I vote for Disneyworld today.'

'No, Seaworld' said Janey quickly. She had caught a quick glimpse of her father's note - a picture of an ear on it, followed by the Sea World logo – and knew *that* was where he wanted her to start her search for Copernicus. Sea World sounded like 'C' World, and it would be just like Copernicus, who was often referred to as The Big C, to turn a place full of sea creatures into C World.

'I want to go to Seaworld,' she repeated.

'Sounds neat to me,' said Alfie, as he joined them for breakfast. He caught Janey's eye and winked.

'Sounds great,' said Jean with a grin, rifling through tourist leaflets. 'We'll get a bus.'

'No need,' said Mrs Halliday, who had now appeared at the table. 'The chauffeur's at our disposal while we're here.'

'This really is the most incredible find.' Jean Brown gathered up her leaflets, shaking her head in pleased bewilderment, and after finishing her breakfast she went off to prepare herself for the day ahead.

Now that the spy team were alone, Mrs Halliday leaned in. 'That was a good bit of advice from your father. Looking for a squid in the ocean, even a mutant one, is a bit like looking for a needle in a haystack …'

'And Sea World is exactly the kind of place The Big C would base his operations.' Janey nodded. 'Let's go.'

'Hang on,' said a voice from Janey's SPIV. 'First thing's first. Get your blonde behind to the villavinivula….la'

'The what?' said Janey.

The SPI:KE tried again. 'The Villa Vanilla,' she intoned slowly. 'That's not easy to say'.

'Will do!' said Janey, and G-Mamma's face disappeared from view. Just then Janey caught sight of her mum coming back from their villa. 'Hey Mum! Just realised I forgot my…er…hat! Back in a mo'.'

Janey raced into the pistachio-coloured villa and pelted upstairs. The vanilla villa was next door, and she'd had an idea of how to get inside, without being seen by her mum.

She flung open the French doors and ran out onto the little balcony. There was a matching one in all the villas, including the vanilla one …

Janey jumped as high as she could and smacked her feet against the balcony floor. Bang! With a familiar little explosion, her Four-Fs launched her into the air. Tucking her head under, Janey vaulted over her own balcony, somersaulted towards the next, and landed neatly on the Villa Vanilla balcony. She peered in the glass and the door swung open. 'Retinal recognition. Great!'

As Janey entered the Spylab that covered the whole of the first floor of the villa, she heard an unmistakable 'miaow' – and her heart leapt. Trouble was here! G-mamma must have SATISPIed him over to Florida! Janey gave him a quick stroke and a hug, then pointed to the cat flap at the bottom of the French doors. 'This is your home while we're here. Have a swim if you want, but don't act like you know us.'

The spycat blinked his green eyes at her, taking in every word, then stalked off in search of further entertainment. As quickly as she could, Janey sprang back to her villa and ran out of the front door, grabbing her PERSPIRE on the way.

'Sorry, couldn't find it,' she explained breathlessly as her mother looked pointedly at her watch.

Jean glanced past her at something strolling along the hedge. 'Good grief. Look at that cat – it's exactly like the one …'

'Let's go!' chorused Alfie, Mrs Halliday and Janey, and with a quick nod of his capped head, Ronnie the chauffeur eased out through the gates and swung the car onto the highway.

It was very useful having a driver who knew his way around Orlando (and was probably armed with some useful spy-buys, Janey guessed). Cooing over the wide boulevards, the palms trees and the melting blaze of sunshine, the Villa Del Sol guests sat back in the car and enjoyed the ride, and within a short space of time they pulled up at the turnstiles ushering them into the exotic land of Sea World.

Alfie burst through the turnstile first, clutching his map. 'Look at all these white-knuckle rides! Yesss! Let's do Atlantis first.'

'Job to do, Alfie,' said Mrs Halliday in an undertone, striding along behind him.

Janey crouched down and spread the park map on her lap. It was really a shame they were on a mission; there was so much to see – the mysterious manatees that sailors used to mistake for mermaids, the dolphins and seals who performed regularly throughout the day. But they had to focus, pick up on Copernicus's trail quickly. And as soon as Janey saw one particular word, she knew where they ought to go.

'How about Shamu, the *killer* whale?' she asked innocently. .'

Jean agreed readily, as Alfie and his mother gave Janey an identical sharp-eyed look and then nodded. They set off across the park, traipsing through the blistering heat, and eventually arrived at Shamu's Happy Harbour.

'Shamu's show is in twenty minutes,' said Jean, studying the agenda. 'Let's see that and then think about getting some lunch. Or at least a drink. I'm exhausted already.'

Mrs Halliday was fanning herself with her handbag, also looking rather wilted; even Alfie was wiping his forehead and puffing loudly every few minutes. Janey was the only one standing up the heat. They shuffled up to the ticket booth and took their seats around the pool, while the arena filled up with tourists.

Suddenly there was a blast of music, and two keepers stepped out onto the platform beyond the pool, waving with both hands and smiling broadly. 'Welcome,' one of them called through his microphone, 'to Shamu's Happy Harbour!'

The crowd clapped and whooped, but then quietened down as the other keeper said, 'But it's not as happy as usual today, is it, Ben?'

'It's not, Jeremy. Shall we tell the audience why?'

Ben the Keeper nodded and turned to the crowd. 'We've got a bit of sad news for ya. Shamu isn't feeling so good today.'

A disappointed 'Awww' rippled across the audience.

'That's right, Ben. We don't think Shamu can come out to play today.'

'Booooo,' called someone in the crowd. Jeremy and Ben suddenly grinned and turned to each other. 'D'ye hear that, Jeremy? I think our friends will be sad if they don't get some entertainment here today.'

Ben nodded, as if he'd suddenly thought of something. 'Hey, how 'bout we bring out Helios instead?'

'We could do,' said Jeremy slowly. 'Whaddya think, guys? Should we bring out , our brand-new killer whale?'

The odd person clapped and cheered, and then suddenly a chant filtered down from the back of the arena. 'Bring out Helios. Bring out Helios.'

'It's his first time…' warned Ben the Keeper.

'Helios! Helios!'

Janey joined in, clapping her hands, while Alfie frowned and sighed. 'Helios,' he muttered. 'I think you'll find that's Greek for *sun*.'

Janey gasped as Helios appeared and arced through the air causing a splash that drenched the first row. *The Sun King*, she thought. That was one of the name's that the power-mad Copernicus had bestowed upon himself.

The killer whale plunged back into the pool in a deluge that soaked all of the front three rows. Jean wiped her dripping face. 'Well, at least I feel a bit cooler now,' she said.

Janey's spy instincts tingled. A new killer whale – named for Copernicus, performing for the first time, on the very day that the spy team came to see the show? And two minutes later, as she stared, terrified, into the open jaws of a killer whale, she knew just what her instincts were trying to tell her.

Chapter 5 Dining with Helios

Copernicus had trained this killer whale to kill Jane Blonde. And right now, Helios had launched himself right out the pool, and was aiming straight for Janey's group. Its terrifying, needle-teethed jaws were wide open. Janey was almost mesmerized by the cavernous depths of the whale's mouth.

And then she snapped into action.

'Out of the way!' She pushed her mother along the water-soaked bench and Mrs Brown slithered to the end where she collapsed in a bundle on the floor. Mrs Halliday rushed to her side while Alfie helped Janey upend the bench and wedged it inside the fast-approaching, murderous mouth. But in seconds Helios's jaws snapped together and shattered the bench into splinters, but it gave Janey enough time to sprint past the whale, vault the tangled remains of the metal-and-perspex guard-rail that was supposed to separate the whale from the audience, and jump into the pool.

'Janey!' Alfie screamed, but Janey was only aware of one thing – she had to get rid of that whale before it got rid of her. Permanently. She glanced around from the middle of the pool, and was thrilled to see Helios had turned around. She really was turning herself into fish bait.

Janey looked feverishly from side to side. Then she looked down.

She took a deep breath and turned turtle, diving for the bottom of the pool. As soon as she was out of sight, Janey grabbed her SPI Direct Energy Replenishment gadget from a concealed pocket in her gold SPIsuit and slipped the rubbery SPIDER into her mouth. At least she could now breathe under water. Helios must have entered the pool through some kind of gate, which probably led through to another holding pool. Maybe she could trap him in there? She swam away not a moment too soon as Helios sliced through the water towards her, hardly able to believe that his prey had leapt into the pool with him and was sitting on the bottom, practically asking to be eaten.

Janey waited until the whale drew near and opened its jaws again. At just at the right moment she planted her feet against Helios's nose and bounced as hard as she could. Her Four-Fs detonated; Helios shot back, emitting a low, cow-like bellow. Janey rattled along the bottom of the pool. There was the gate! Janey raced up to it and clung on to the close-set iron bars, but there was no way through . She felt her way along the side of the pool, feeling rather than seeing that Helios had recovered himself and was once more headed straight for her. She had only moments. Was she going to get eaten? Or was she going to act like a spylet? *Die or Spy*, she thought grimly.

Then suddenly she saw it. An underwater window! Through it she could see some sort of restaurant, and the words 'Dine with Shamu' written on an overhanging sign. The room was empty. Helios's black and red mouth loomed. With not a moment to spare, Janey wrenched off her left Four-F and looked for the button that would operate the circular saw. There! Aa tiny 'S' in a circle at the point at which the straps crossed over. She pressed. She prayed.   And she was flung backwards k as the Four-F suddenly whizzed around in her hand. The clung onto the strap And watched, amazed, as jagged saw-teeth appeared around the edge of the Four-F.. She held it up to the glass, squinting just long enough to see in the reflective glass that the killer whale's jaws were practically upon her . . . there was a hideous shriek of metal on glass, then a line appeared down the middle of the window, and a million gallons of water pressed against the severed glass causing it to shatter outwards. Water sprayed and shards of tempered glass were blasted all over the dining tables. Janey was rushed along on a gushing torrent of water, straight out under the 'Dine with Shamu' sign. When she turned around, Helios's nose was wedged tightly in the space where the window had been. She'd been very, very close to dining with Helios.

Janey was just picking herself up off the floor when her mother, Alfie and Mrs Halliday skidded into the room. 'Janey!' Jean Brown swept her up in an enormous embrace, while Alfie shouted, 'She's okay. She's down here,' to the very anxious Ben and Jeremy at the top of the stairs.

Ben wrung his hands, his face white with fear. 'We are so … so sorry! We've called for medical attention for you, and … Helios … we have to get him back in the other tank, and we will never, I repeat NEVER again, use a whale we haven't trained ourselves.'

'So when did Helios arrive?' asked Mrs Halliday.

'His trainers brought him in a day or two ago – they said he'd been reared in captivity.'

'Well, you better make sure you have him safely locked up.' said Janey. 'And don't worry – it was just an accident. Could have happened to anyone.'

'NOT,' said Alfie under his breath.

The four of them slopped out of the restaurant 'Are you sure you're all right, Janey?' asked her mum. 'You were under water for so long. You might have suffered loss of oxygen to your brain. How did that glass break? Why did you jump in the pool? Honestly, my heart nearly fell out of my mouth.' Jean kept up a stream of questions and statements of horror until they were once more out in the sunshine. 'What a bizarre, terrible thing to happen,' she said finally, making Janey sit down on a dolphin-shaped seat.

Funny how they always happen to me, thought Janey. She pulled her mum down next to her. 'I'm fine. I just … panicked and went the wrong way. But I'm not even hurt, honestly.'

She held up her gold-covered limbs for her mother to inspect, and finally Jean sat back, satisfied but still trembling. 'I definitely need a cup of tea now,' she said weakly.

It was exactly what they needed – a chance to get back to the Spylab and report in to Abe. 'Good idea,' said Mrs Halliday. Let's get back to the villas and relax around the pool.'

All in agreement, they began the long walk back to the turnstiles and to Ronnie, who was waiting for them, as promised.

They collapsed gratefully into the air-conditioned car interior. 'That sun is just *melting*,' said Alfie, flopping out his tongue and panting like a dog.

'I've never been so hot,' agreed Mrs Halliday. 'That last thirty yards were torture.'

Janey's mum propped her head up on her hand. 'Exhausted. Going to have to carry … a parasol.'

'What is wrong with you all?' Janey looked round at them all from the seat beside Ronnie. 'I'm the one who just had a close encounter with a killer beast.'

But that didn't seem to matter. 'Tea,' said Mrs Halliday in a hoarse and longing whisper.

And tea it was, followed by a long lie-down by the pool, and more tea and cold lemonade in the mid-afternoon. Janey paced between the sun loungers, trying to motivate the others. How could they just relax when Copernicus was obviously so close? They had to get on with finding him, with ensuring the safety of her dad's Revolution secret. Whatever his Revolution secret *was*. But it was no use so she went inside, then popped straight out of the French windows from the back bedroom, over the balcony, and into the Villa Vanilla Spylab.

'Hey, Trouble,' she said, giving the cat a rub behind the ears. He was still a bit damp from having a paddle around the pool while they were out. Sitting down next to him at the workbench, Janey tapped into the computer and accessed G-Mamma.

'Blonde,' yelled her SPI:KE 'give me the lowdown.'

'I've just been attacked by a killer whale, and Copernicus is behind it,' She said matter-of-factly.

G-Mamma's round eyes doubled in size. '

'Whopping whales, I'll let you're the boss man know immediately! In fact, I've just been talking to your father.' G-Mamma leaned into the screen furtively. 'He says Copernicus is behind the disappearance of a few other animals from Solfari Lands. It's like he's baiting your father. Stealing from him so brazenly . '

'What kind of animals?' asked Janey.

'I don't want to say in case someone's listening in with a SPI-pod . But I'll act it out for you.' With that, G-Mamma moved away from the screen so Janey could see her in full. Then she pointed towards her waist, and mimed great surprise by making her eyes and mouth very round.

'Er, sorry, I didn't get that.'

Again G-Mamma pointed towards her waist and then looked very surprised.

'Waist …shock.' Janey shrugged. What on earth could that mean?

'No! And don't say it out loud, Janey Zaney.' Once more she stuck out a finger and waved it at her waist, but this time she let it come to rest just below her belt, and to the side.

'Ah!' Janey got it. Hip. But what was the other bit? She watched G-Mamma's mouth go round, and suddenly it came to her. Oh. Hip. Oh. Hippo. The animals going missing, were hippos!

'How many?' she said after giving G-Mamma to show she'd understood.

'All eleven of the Solfari Lands hippos.'

Janey thought for a moment. Monkeys missing, hippos disappearing, and killer whales attacking. What could it all mean? 'It's time we got to the bottom of this, G-mamma. Dad's counting on us - but everyone's so jet-lagged at the moment, I feel like I'm on my own.'

'Well not for long,' snapped G-Mamma, as Janey left to re-join the group by the pool.

G-Mamma was true to her word, as an hour later, the Villa del Sol gates swung open and Ronnie nosed the car through. Janey, Alfie and their mothers all sat up to see what was going on, just as a large figure in a florid, flouncy sundress clambered out of the front seat.

'It's me!' declared G-Mamma brightly. 'Goodness, what a coincidence. Fancy me and the kids landing in *exactly* the same holiday villas as you. We're in the coffee-coloured one, right?'

45

She pulled open the back door of the car. 'Come on, kids! Come and meet the neighbours.'

And to Janey's great astonishment, two children stepped sheepishly from the car: Tish, in a red SPIsuit like Janey's, and Leaf in green board shorts and rash shirt like Alfie's.

G-Mamma beamed. 'Oh, aren't we all going to have FUN! Now, did I see a tea-pot?'

Having helped herself to a flagon of tea, G-Mamma installed herself and her two spylets in the coffee-coloured villa while Jean Brown hissed questions at Janey.

'How on earth did that mad woman from next door end up here? Whose children are those? Did you hear them? They don't even have the same accents. Do you think we should alert the authorities? And where did she find that dress?'

Janey held up her hands, as if in defeat. How could she explain it all to her mum? 'Rosie Biggenham,' said Mrs Halliday casually. 'Fancy her turning up like that. She used to be a teacher at one of my old schools, you know, Jean. The kids all loved her – she left to start fostering children. Those must be two of her foster-children, back for a holiday. Very big ... um ... heart, that woman has.'

Alfie headed off for a dip in the pool, hissing, 'Very big *everything*.

Jean Brown shook her head, blinking rapidly. 'Well, to be honest I see quite enough of her at home, without her turning up on our holiday like this. I'm sure she's very nice and everything …'

'She is very nice,' said Janey. 'You should try to get to know her a bit more.' And I should be able to get on with my mission, now that I've got some more back-up, she thought.

But Janey was sadly disappointed. The new arrivals emerged from the coffee-coloured villa in their sun and swimming gear, G-Mamma sporting a large floral swimming cap that made her head look like a sea anemone. Grabbing a lounger each, they stretched out to have a chat with their new neighbours, tipping sun-cream over themselves, only for Janey to find that the conversation stopped within fifteen minutes. Everyone, except Leaf, had dropped off, and lay sprawled out like cats in the sunshine. 'I know we're meant to relax,' she said softly to Leaf as she looked round at the sleeping forms around them, 'but this is just pathetic.'

He shrugged. 'They are just not used to sun this strong. Where I come from, in the summer it is bright sunshine until three o'clock in the morning, so I am very used to it.'

'Well, I'm not,' said Janey, 'but I seem to be okay.'

'They are just not as strong as we are, Blonde,' said Leaf. 'Volleyball?'

The spylets batted a ball around in the pool. While Leaf explained that they had gathered their spy-gear together as soon as Janey had spoken with G-Mamma, and SATISPIed over to the Florida Spylab. Then they had had to sneak out of the back of the villa, climb into the car and make their official entrance through the front gate. 'Father is still working with Mr Rownigan on this Revolution process, and we have left the protection of Solfari Lands to the Bird family.'

'Is that safe?' said Janey, who still didn't fully trust Blackbird.

Leaf shrugged. 'How much of this is ever safe?'

'True.' Leaf was right. Theirs was not a very safe world at all. And she'd dragged her mum right into the middle of it, trying to give her a holiday. Blackbird was definitely not the only one who made 'errors of judgement'.

As twilight fell, the two spylets finally managed to wake up the other members of their party, and they all sat around the barbecue trying to make polite conversation while Mrs Halliday and Alfie assembled hot-dogs and passed them around. 'One or two?' said Mrs Halliday to Tish. 'Four, please,' called G-Mamma before Tish had chance to open her mouth. 'All that traveling has worn me out. In fact,' she said with a gigantic yawn, 'I must have jet lag. Straight to bed after this snack.'

Straight to bed. Janey almost smirked. G-Mamma was making an excuse, covering for them so that they could all get off to bed early, meet up in the Spylab and begin a serious search and destroy campaign on Copernicus. A

48

little thrill ran through her; soon, the mission would be properly underway.

G-Mamma was as good as her word. As soon as the last onion shred had been scooped off the plate, she nodded at Tish and Leaf. 'Beddy bye-byes for weary travellers. Come on, kidlets – you snooze or you lose.'

Janey stood up quickly.

'Me too!' she stretched her arms. 'I'm pretty tired – didn't have a long nap like the rest of you. I think I'll go up to bed as well.'

Everybody else levered themselves off their chairs at the same time. 'I'm still quite tired,' said Jean, rubbing her eyes.

'Yes, today was quite … challenging,' agreed Mrs Halliday. 'We can wash up in the morning.'

Alfie stared. 'Are you feeling all right?' he said to his mother. 'We never leave the washing up.'

But Mrs Halliday just waved her hand. 'We're on holiday, Alfie. I can't summon up the energy to care about it.'

They all said goodnight and sloped off to their respective villas, Janey pretending she was going straight to bed too. She hopped around in her room until she was sure her mother would be asleep, then sneaked out on the balcony to vault across to the Spylab. apart from Trouble cleaning his paws on the computer bench, the place was completely empty. To fill in the time while she waited for the others, Janey chatted to Trouble as she stroked his tawny head before sending him into the Wower. 'We're off on a mission,' she told him as she stowed a new SPIDER in her pocket, got her new ASPIC ready, and added a golden Girl-Gauntlet to her summer spysuit. After twenty minutes, however, there was still no sign of anyone else.

With a sigh, Janey Four-F'd her way across the back balconies to get to Alfie's room. Through the French windows, she could see him sprawled at an angle across the bed; it looked as though he'd barely made it into the room before collapsing across it.

'Alfie!' Janey tapped on the window. 'Wake up!'

He didn't stir, so she moved along the balcony to the next windows. Mrs Halliday was also fast asleep, and no amount of door rattling was going to wake her.

The picture was very much the same at G-Mamma's. It looked as though the SPI:KE had fallen asleep half-way through taking off her make-up, spread-eagled at the dressing table. Janey knocked on the glass. 'G-Mamma!' There was a brief snort as G-Mamma shifted in her seat, but that was all.

Janey had had enough. 'Trouble, sabre-claw your way through this window,' she instructed, pointing to the little pane of glass directly below the door handle. Trouble didn't need to be asked twice, and he flicked open the biggest claw on his front paw. It curved towards the door like a pirate's cutlass, and in seconds Trouble had stripped out the putty holding in the glass so the pane dropped out onto Janey's outstretched, Girl-Gauntlet-protected hand in one piece.

Janey ran to G-Mamma's side. 'Wake up,' she said urgently, shaking her SPI:KE's shoulder. 'Come on!' Nothing seemed to stir her. Janey changed tack and crooned directly into the G-Mamma's ear. ' I've got doughnuts.'

G-Mamma sat up with a start, one eye still surrounded with Perfect Purple eye-dazzle, the other clean, small and beady. For a second Janey was reminded of Copernicus's mismatched eyes – one human, one yellow and monstrous. 'Whaddya … where?' said G-Mamma blearily.

'Come on,' said Janey. 'We've got to track down Copernicus.'

'Does he have the doughnuts?'

Janey nearly stamped her foot with frustration as her SPIK:E's eyes closed.

It was no use. Janey couldn't believe it. Another night wasted.

'Perfect,' she said bitterly. 'On my own again.'

Except I'm not, thought Janey as she logged into the Spylab computer. Her dad would know what to do. It was time to ask him directly for help. Then tomorrow she'd be able to start the search – with or without the team.

Chapter 7 The river of grass

D o I look like a hippo-hunter?' yawned G-Mamma. Janey looked at the tired faces grouped around the Spylab. She'd managed to wake everyone at dawn, after she'd received an email from her dad. He wanted them to locate the missing hippos – immediately. 'My dad said we have to,' she told them firmly. 'Find a river, find the hippos.' It was a clear directive, and the snoozing spies were not going to wriggle out of it.

Once the grumbling spy team had agreed to meet for breakfast in five minutes, Janey jumped over the balcony and into her bedroom just as she heard her mum come out of her bedroom.

'Up already?' Jean's tousled head appeared around the door. 'Janey, I think you should change out of that gold swimsuit thing. And take that hat off. You've been wearing them non-stop since we set off.'

Janey looked down at her Spysuit. 'But … it's really comfy,' she said pleadingly. 'And I do keep swimming in it, so it's clean and everything.'

'You know, I'm just wondering,' said her mother, staring again at Janey's golden outfit, 'where you got it from anyway. I don't remember buying it for you.'

'Mrs Halliday got it when she bought Alfie's.' Janey smiled to cover up the enormous lie she had once more told her mother. Inwardly she sighed. It would be so nice to be able to tell her the truth.

'Okay,' said her mother. 'Well, let's see if Mad Rosie's managed breakfast this morning.'

'Oh, I'm sure she has.'

She pushed her mum ahead of her along the landing, and together they made their way out into the bright lemony yellow of the morning. It was already warm, and G-Mamma was glowing as she flipped fried eggs on the barbecue griddle. 'Sunny side up,' she carolled as Janey took a plate. 'Just right for Florida. Although, jeepers, it's hot! Next time I'm doing breakfast we're having ice cream.'

'So what's the plan?' Jean added some bacon to her eggs and sat down at the large wooden table, adding hopefully, 'Disneyworld, maybe?'

The group hummed and hawed reluctantly. 'I think it may be a bit hot to walk around a theme park,' said Mrs Halliday.

'I vote for somewhere natural,' said Leaf.

Tish nodded enthusiastically. 'Oh, I love … natural things. How about somewhere with a … I don't know … a river?'

'Sounds good to me,' said Alfie quickly.

'Great idea!' said Janey, who was quickly flicking through her mum's collection of tourist attraction leaflets. 'Let's go to the Everglades!' she shouted, a little too loudly, as she flicked past one particular leaflet. 'It's meant to be really interesting, Mum,' she added, more quietly.

Everyone agreed The Everglades would be perfect and very soon the chauffeur driven car pulled into the driveway. Ronnie got out of the car, mopping his brow with a great yellow handkerchief. 'Where to today, folks?' he said breathlessly. 'The Everglades please,' said Janey eagerly.

Ronnie's chubby face stretched into a smile. 'Ah, The River of Grass,' he said with a slow nod. 'You'll have a lot of fun there. Just watch out for gaters.'

'What are gaters?' Tish asked as she climbed into the very back seat with Leaf and Alfie.

Ronnie held the door as Janey, her mum and Mrs Halliday got into the middle seat and G-Mamma eased herself into the passenger seat next to the driver. 'You'll see,' he said with a grin. 'It's a real long drive, so I'll take you to the airport and we'll fly there. All courtesy of Villa Del Sol.'

Half an hour later they were boarding a small plane, that bobbed on a little lake near by the tiny airport. Janey glanced at the two floats beneath the fuselage.

'Cool!' said Alfie, breathlessly..

'This holiday package is just … unbelievable,' Jean Brown muttered.   Janey squeezed her arm. 'Are you having a good time, Mum?'

'The best!' Jean held up her hands. 'Even with Dozy Rosie from next door.' And she smiled happily as she buckled her seat belt.

The plane ride was uneventful, apart from a small loop-the-loop when an ecstatic Alfie was invited up the cockpit by Ronnie – who it turned out was a pilot as well as a driver – and soon they were landing among lush greenery of The Everglades, on a wide and murky river.

'I am seeing why they call it the River of Grass,' said Leaf, almost disappearing from view as they disembarked onto a narrow walkway and his green spy-suit blended with the vegetation.

'Keep your toes away from the edge,' called Ronnie from the front of the line. 'We don't want those 'gators to have them.'

'Janey looked down at the water, and sure enough, a knobbled, sinuous body was slipping away from the walkway into the reeds. She definitely planned on staying out of *their* way . . .

Ronnie led the way, pointing out various features, then as they reached a gate to a small enclosure, he stopped suddenly. 'Sorry, folks, just got a bit hot and bothered there,' he panted. 'That's better . . . and here's your next method of transportation.'

He pointed over the gate to a strange contraption parked at the riverside. It looked rather like a small stage with a cage at the back, balanced high above some enormous inflated tank tyres.

Alfie drew in a sharp breath, like a backwards sigh. 'Swamp buggy,' he crooned, hardly able to speak. 'Pontoon bodywork, racing engine, big flat flotation tyres, paddle treads on the rear for the forward motion, rudder-steering …'

He stumbled over the flattened gross towards the vehicle, but G-Mamma swiped him across the head with her large floral PERSPIRE. 'Oi, Petrolhead,' she barked. 'Ladies first.'

The swamp buggy rocked dangerously as G-Mamma climbed aboard, handed across by Ronnie, then the others slotted themselves into the seats that were bolted onto the floor. 'Strap yourselves in, and hold tight!' yelled Ronnie.

The engine whined, spluttered into action, and then burst into life with a roar like a caged animal released from its prison. Janey clutched Alfie's arm as they skated across the surface of the river at forty miles an hour, flattening reeds and shooting out frothy wakes like milkshakes as they careered around bends in the river.

'I have got to get one of these!' said Alfie, his face radiant with joy.

Janey took in as much as she could as Ronnie whipped them around the river, screaming as if they were on a roller coaster. It certainly looked tropical enough for hippos. Suddenly the engine note changed and the buggy slowed down.

'We're right in the heart of 'gator land now,' said Ronnie softly, bringing the swamp buggy to a stop for a moment. 'Look around, folks.'

They all did as they were told. At first the river looked uninhabited, calm even, but then Ronnie tossed a lump of steak over the side, and the water around them began to boil. One, two … many sets of long, evil-teethed jaws broke the surface, like monstrous baby birds snapping for food, and all around, glinting in the sunlight that danced through the tree-tops, was a writhing, thrashing mass of reptilian killers. One even managed to reach up to the edge of the platform, snapping ferociously. Janey stared in horror at the long, clawed foot, so like a deformed human hand …

G-Mamma leaned forward and hissed in Janey's ear. 'Compared with this lot, old Copper Knickers is a pussy-cat! I think I'm a 'gator-hater.'

Janey just nodded, then she glanced back at Ronnie, urging him to move on. The sweat was running off his forehead and down his cheeks but after wiping his face on his sleeve, he revved up the engine again. 'That sun's a scorcher,' he said, 'even through the trees. Let's head for one of the camps and grab ourselves some lunch.'

'Before something grabs *us* for lunch,' said Tish with a cheery, gap-toothed grin.

The sun beat down on them as they found their way to the picnic tables, safely fenced off from the river bank with the odd cypress tree creating scant shade. Everyone fell upon the picnic with gusto, tearing into the fried chicken legs and great chunky sandwiches with the same fervor that the alligators had just displayed over the steak. The meal was rounded up with more doughnuts than even G-Mamma could manage, and washed down with gallons of fresh, cool water.

Jean stretched. 'That was lovely. Funny how it's so relaxing, even with those alligators so close by.'

'It's a real holiday, isn't it, Jean?' agreed Mrs Halliday, lying down full length on one of the blankets they'd spread on the ground. 'I could do with a nap.'

Ronnie looked delighted. 'If you folks all want a siesta, that's fine by me. This heat's got me beat today.'

'Sticky buns, sweaty suns … heat's got me beat …' yawned G-Mamma. 'I'd make up a rap if I had the energy. Hmm, sticky bu …'

She stopped abruptly. Janey couldn't believe it: G-Mamma had simply fallen asleep. Alfie had been sketching swamp buggies on his napkin, but his head was now nodding towards the table. 'Five minutes,' he mumbled incoherently. 'Power nap…' Everyone had decided to take full advantage of siesta time, apart from Leaf who was packing up the picnic hamper.

Well she wasn't going to waste any more time. She had a plan. 'I'm going to take another look around,' she said to Leaf.

His eyes followed hers down to the riverbank. 'Take care,' he said. 'I will keep look out for everyone here.'

Janey grabbed the bag of steak, and approached the riverbank cautiously.

'Okay, 'gators, let's get you out of the way,' she whispered, before tearing a hole in the plastic bag of meat and lobbing it as far away as she could, towards the far bank of the river. Almost instantly, three of four alligators emerged from the water, lured by the scent of the steak, and swam away from Janey.. She made her way carefully into the reeds, looking for clues of some kind. Hippo poo? She wouldn't be able to tell it apart from alligator poo. She'd been searching for over half an hour before she came across something that might be significant.

It was a foot-print: a wide, splayed, four-toed footprint the size of a dinner plate. Janey studied it carefully. It certainly didn't look like a print made by the shrivelled claw of an alligator. …

She took off her PERSPIRE, turned it over, and pressed the tiny button at the centre of the cap.

Instantly, a tiny touch-screen keyboard was projected onto the underside of the cap's peak, and the inside glowed white like a ghostly television screen. 'Okay.' Janey typed in the words 'Hippo foot' and waited.

An image popped up onto the screen – a four-toed foot, with toes splayed left and right and two facing forwards. She looked at the footprint next to her. It was an exact match.

'Where do hippos live?' she tapped in next.

''Hippos are found in sub-Saharan Africa,'' she read, 'where they are largely considered to be the most dangerous wild animal of all, weighing up to 800 pounds and capable of running speeds of twenty miles an hour.'' Janey glanced at her Fleet-Feet Flip-Flops. 'Well, I'm faster than that.'

She popped her PERSPIRE back on and returned to the picnic area where Leaf, still the only one awake, was whittling a piece of wood into the shape of an alligator.

'Dad was right,' said Janey quietly, straining to be heard above the cacophony of snorts and snores that filled the air. 'There are hippos here, and they aren't usually found living in the wild in America.'

Leaf looked around at their sleeping companions.. He shrugged. 'There is not much we can do at the moment.'

But Jane Blonde wasn't used to waiting when there was a mission at hand. 'There is something we can do. *Cover for me,*' she said, and headed into the thickly-knotted mangroves.

Chapter 8 Terrifying teeth

Janey found her way back to the hippopotamus footprint, hoping to find another – a neat, obliging little trail of prints that would lead her directly to the stolen hippos. What she did find was rather more alarming: two sets of claw marks, raked into the mud, with a sweep of mud between them. An alligator had been on this bank since her last visit, and had slid back into the water, possibly dragging a hippo. And if it could drag a hippo, it could certainly topple Jane Blonde. Topple her, seize her in its jaws, and crunch her to Blonde-dust. She had to be quick.

Janey scanned the area. 'Where are they?'

Suddenly she thought of something – an easy way to make the footprints appear to her, without having to rummage around in the alligator-infested mangroves looking for them. Pulling of her PERSPIRE, she brought up the image of the four-toed hippo print, then focused her Ultra-gogs on it. 'Match,' she said firmly. 'Match and find.'

She put her hat back on, and turned slowly on the spot, allowing her Ultra-gogs to scan the area for footprints. Suddenly her spy-glasses gave a beep and zoomed in on an image. Janey looked excitedly. 'It worked' she cried. 'And again. Match and find.'

As she scanned further along the bank, the Ultra-gogs whirred, clicked into focus, and then emitted a loud 'BEEEEEEP.'

'Perfect!' Janey slithered along to the next footprint. It was still only one on its own, but if the Ultra-gogs could keep 'matching and finding', she'd be bound to come across a whole hippo soon …

She lurched from one footprint to the next. Occasionally she would find two prints, and imagine excitedly that the hippo was just beyond the next mangrove tree, only to find the next print, half-submerged in water.

Eventually, as Janey looked upwards for the first time and noticed that it was getting dark, she started to feel worried. Perhaps she was never going to find this hippo. Maybe someone – some enemy spy – had laid a trail for her, luring her further and further away from her spy team. She looked back the way she had just come, and her heart sank. How far had she travelled? What if she got lost? 'Match and find,' said Janey once more, trying to gather her courage by focusing on the job in hand.

She turned her head this way and that, waiting, hoping for the bright BEEP which signified a new footprint. But the Ultra-gogs were completely silent. And then Janey saw them.

Four alligators were swinging their monstrous bodies through the mangroves, their flat heads parting the grasses like chain saws, evil green-gold eyes glowing in the gathering gloom. The colour of their skin was so mud-like that were it not for the glint of their eyes, Janey would hardly have seen them …

Then they opened their mouths, and Janey realised the beasts were moving in for the kill. For a moment, she was too stunned to do anything. Then she jumped.

Flinging herself up in the air, Janey brought her knees up to her chest and slammed her feet back down against the floor, hoping that she didn't slip over in the mud and deliver herself into the nearest cavernous mouth. Her feet met the ground only briefly, and she staggered slightly as the Four F's detonated beneath her and launched her towards the sky like a firework.

Unfortunately, her slight stumble at take-off meant that she'd been launched at an angle, an angle that had directed her away from the bank, and straight into the murky middle of the river.

'Oh no,' said Janey. She had no Girl Gauntlet, no ASPIC – in fact, no way of escaping the alligators' jaws of death as she fell into the Everglades. And she'd brought it all on herself, assuming once more that Jane Blonde, even on her own, could do anything.

The water rushed up to meet her and her feet hit the surface . . .

And stayed there.

She opened her eyes. I'm walking on water, she thought.

Janey couldn't believe what she was seeing – it was a miracle. She seemed to be standing on something solid , yet she could feel water all around her feet. Meanwhile, the alligators had spotted her and with a flick of their loathsome tails, they were headed straight for her.

Janey ran, her feet splashing across the surface as her Four Fs would allow her. It felt like she was leaping across a strange causeway, until, with a sob of relief, she hit dry land on the far riverbank.

'Zoom,' she said, her heart beating wildly. The alligators had not kept chase – but something was close by. An eye blinked malevolently from the water, reflecting the shimmer from the rising moon. Janey zoomed in once more with her Ultra-gogs. To her astonishment a round ear, rather like a teddy bear's but without the fur, had risen up above the water near the eye. And there was another set of eyes. . . and another.

Janey swallowed hard as the nearest set of eyes moved closer. She peered into the water, hardly able to believe what she was seeing.

The causeway she had run across was breaking up. Parts were paddling downstream, while other bits of it were lining up and approaching the river bank. Fast. She hadn't been walking on water after all. Jane Blonde had simply had the good luck to land on the back of a submerged hippopotamus, had run across onto the back of the next, and had managed to stretch right the way across on a walkway of hippos, lurking just under the surface of the water.

Only now they were coming for her. What was it the PERSPIRE had told her? Hippos were known as the most dangerous African animal? They looked so cute at the zoo, but as one clambered purposefully out of the water, lowered its head, and opened its enormous mouth wide, Janey suddenly remembered the rest of the information. They weighed 3,600 kgs, and ran at 20 miles an hour. She was about to be chased by ... she counted quickly ... eleven of the world's most deadly animals. Then just as she felt the ground shudder beneath the weight of the attacking hippos, Janey heard a sound that lifted her heart – a splutter and a roar of engines, then the cry of her best friend and fellow spylet: 'Blonde! Get ready to jump!'

The swamp buggy blasted around the bend through the gathering darkness, lights blazing and engine roaring. Tish and Leaf were leaning off the front of the buggy, Girl Gauntlet and Boy Battler at the ready. Alfie, meanwhile, was hanging onto the rudder with both hands, zig-zagging across the river.

'Three,' he hollered, so loudly that Janey realised he must be shouting into the MIC setting on his SPI-Pod. 'Two.' The buggy swerved into its final lunge towards Janey. 'One. NOW.'

Just as the swamp buggy slid sideways towards her, two more hippo heads emerged from the water. Taking off from the slippery riverbank, she planted a foot on each head, right between the teddy-like ears, and vaulted off them towards the boat. Tish and Leaf each reached out to grab one of her hands, and in the next second Janey was lying in a crumpled pile between the buggy's seats.

'Blonde!' Alfie pulled away, dodging hippos and alligators. His face was alight with joy and excitement.

'What?' asked Janey, who was more than a little dazed.

'This baby,' he said, patting the rudder beneath his hand, 'drives like an absolute DREAM.'

Janey rolled her eyes. 'Right,' she said. 'Nice to see you too.'

Chapter 9 Tired old tiger

They arrived back at the Villa Del Sol sometime after midnight, with Janey holding her mother's hand the whole way. Jean had woken up to find her daughter had disappeared; convinced she had been dragged away by alligators, she had screamed so loud that everyone woke up Leaf quickly explained that Janey had just gone to the toilet, and when Tish and Alfie had realised what was going on, they insisted that they needed to go too. Then the spylets had made straight for Ronnie's swamp buggy. While they were gone, Mrs Halliday and G-Mamma calmly packed the picnic gear, and fielded Jean Brown's questions.

Now Janey wished for the millionth time since she'd become a spylet that she could just tell her mother the truth. Instead she settled for making sure Jean was asleep, getting across to the Spylab, and telling the others about her discoveries.

'They were all there,' she said to the assembled SPI:KEs and spylets. 'Eleven hippos, just lying around in the Everglades.'

'I know how they felt,' said G-Mamma, her eye make-up smudged after her afternoon-long nap. 'You have to fight the heat,' said Janey. 'You're right, Janey,' said Mrs Halliday. 'But right now it's night-time, and we're all a bit more alert. What's our plan?'

Tish stuck up her hand. 'How about Satispying back to the Everglades, rounding up those hippos and sending them back to Solfari Lands.'

Leaf apparently agreed. 'I will volunteer to go back to the Everglades tonight.'

'I'll come with you.' Janey pulled a Girl Gauntlet from a cupboard. She wasn't going without full protection this time.

'Me too,' said G-Mamma. 'And Tish, seeing as it was her idea.'

It was agreed that they would be the hippo party, while Alfie and Mrs Halliday would watch out for Jean Brown, alert Abe Rownigan, and operate the Satispy remote control. Seconds later, the three spylets zapped down in the swamp, a traffic light of red, gold and green spy-suits, followed by G-Mamma in shimmering grey. When she shoved a SPIDER in her mouth and lowered herself under the water, she looked rather like a hippo herself. 'Come on … bloop burple,' she called as her mouth filled with water, waggling her eyebrows to signify that the others should follow.

They submerged themselves, Ultra-gogs on both night and water vision, gloves at the ready to fight off any passing alligators or hippos who were less than keen to go back to the zoo.

After a few minutes groping around in the murky river, the spylets and SPI:KE popped up above the surface. 'Nothing,' said Janey. 'But there were all here.'

68

Leaf nodded. 'We saw them too. How about I just get that swamp-buggy and we check a bit further …'

'Forget it, Leafo,' snapped G-Mamma. 'It's my turn with the boys' toys. Blonde, you come with me. Titian and Leaf, you make for those cypress trees. Any trouble, SPIV me.'

Leaf merely raised an eyebrow, popped his SPIDER back in his mouth, and followed Tish, who was already cutting through the water in a steady and rather impressive crawl. Janey and her SPI:KE climbed aboard the swamp-buggy and blasted off in the other direction, slewing to a halt at intervals so Janey could bob into the water and have a look beneath the surface. Every so often they caught sight of an alligator's tail or a pair of glowing amber eyes, but it became very evident, after several miles had been covered, that the hippos were no longer there.

'Mud, mud, glorious mud,' sang G-Mamma quietly. 'Nothing quite like it for disguising missing hippos … So follow me, follow, down to the hollow, and there let us wallow, because there's absolutely nooooooooothing else there ...'

Janey shrugged her shoulders where the rising sun was beginning to warm them. 'This is hopeless. They've been moved. Copernicus must have found out we were on to them.'

At that moment the SPIV around her neck buzzed into life. Leaf's face appeared, smothering a yawn. 'There is nothing here. We are back at the picnic place, and we have seen a couple of alligators but that is all.' He panned the SPIV around the picnic site to demonstrate. It was completely quiet, apart from the gentle sound of Tish snoring, curled up on a picnic bench. 'We are both very exhausted,' Leaf explained. 'All that swimming …'

G-Mamma's head was Also starting to loll so Janey grabbed the rudder and steered them around in a circle. 'We'll head back to the site,' she told Leaf. 'We might as well go home.'

They SATISPIED back to the familiar welcome of the Villas Del Sol. Mrs Halliday and Alfie passed the details on to Solfari Lands after a brief De-code and De-Wow session as Janey stood under the spy shower, letting the incredible droplets melt away a hard night's spy work. Leaf, Tish and G-Mamma, meanwhile, had simply collapsed on the sun-beds outside their villa and fallen asleep.

An hour later, Jean Brown got up from the breakfast table and angled a parasol over G-Mamma's face. 'She's starting to look like a pumpkin.'

'Ugh,' snorted Alfie. 'Imagine that all carved out with a candle in it. Very Halloween.'

'That's enough.' Mrs Halliday pushed her croissant to one side. 'In fact, even more than that – I think a little dozing in the sun looks like a very good idea. We'll just hang around here today, I think.'

To Janey's surprise, Alfie didn't argue, but simply nodded and yawned. At least now I can get to Disneyworld with Mum, thought Janey. Even spylets need a day off.

Jean Brown was delighted with the suggestion. 'Yes! Great idea, Janey.'

Janey, de-wowed into shorts and a strappy tee-shirt, was soon jumping into the back of the car, and as the ever-obliging Ronnie drove them up to the turnstiles of the Magic Kingdom, her mum jigged up and down on her seat. 'I'm so excited!' she beamed Jean   Janey smiled. If only Jean knew how exciting her own spy-life used to be.   It was tremendous fun. They queued for thrilling rides, waved at various characters, and watched scenes from films re-enacted before their very eyes. By lunchtime Janey was exhausted, and even Jean's enthusiasm seemed to have dwindled. She sank onto a stone toadstool, fanning herself with the guidebook.

'Gosh, it's hot. I might have to go back to the villa for a swim,' she said, sweat trickling from the browband of her hat.

Janey had to agree. All her clothes were sticking to her in a way that her golden Spysuit never did, and a crushing headache gripped her brain so that planning the next event seemed too difficult a task. She peered at the guide. 'The parade's at three. Why don't we sit in the shade until then?'

Her mum agreed, and together they staggered to a refreshment site. Many other people had had the same idea, and the queues for drinks and ice-creams were bigger than some of the queues for the rides. A nice family from Germany took pity on the Browns and allowed them to perch on the end of their shaded table, and Jean revived enough to get food and water for them both.

Janey smiled at the family - mum, dad and two boys about seven years old - as her mum headed towards the counter, bouncing off tables as she went. 'Hot,' she said, fanning her face.

'Ja!' said the mother, pointing to her children. One of the boys was crying listlessly into his fries, and the other was slumped against his father, who had his head propped in his hands as he slurped his super-sized cola.

Looking around, Janey could see that everyone was feeling the same. A family a few tables away was bickering over a water bottle, and a small tussle broke out between the mother and her teenage daughter. Elsewhere everyone was quiet, sticking out their lower lips to blow cooling air over their sticky faces, or fanning themselves with whatever they could get their hands on.

Finally, Jean Brown came back with their lunch. 'That was hard work,' she said breathlessly. 'One of the staff had passed out behind the counter, and the others were just stepping over him, they were so busy.'

'This is mad, Mum,' said Janey, stifling an enormous yawn. 'Why don't we just forget the parade?'

'I want to see Mickey Mouse,' said her mother firmly. 'And Pooh Bear.'

'Okay,' said Janey with a grin. Deep down she really wanted to see them too. And by the time they had finished their salads and bottles of water, and had a little snooze in their seats, it was almost three o'clock anyway …

They lined up with what felt like the rest of America, with hundreds of fractious children and equally ratty adults. There was a lack-lustre cheer as the parade began, and Jean Brown turned a yawn into a grin. 'The Little Mermaid!' she cried, nudging Janey. 'She used to be your favourite. And Cinderella. And … what's that one called?' She stopped, puzzled.

'Snow White,' said Janey.

Jean shook herself. 'Snow White! How could I forget that? It's so hot out here I can hardly think.'

She wasn't the only one, it seemed. Janey peered more closely as the elaborately decorated float with the Little Mermaid on it passed by. The mermaid was asleep, statue-like with her hand in a wave and her head tipped to one side. The other characters were just managing to shuffle along, nodding to the crowd, or perhaps nodding with fatigue, and then Janey spotted her mum's favourite further along the parade.

'Look, Mum,' she said. 'It's Tigger!!'

They both turned in delight, but their expressions turned to horrified bafflement as the famous tiger raised his right paw, tottered for a moment as if he'd lifted something heavy over his head, then careered right with little stumbling steps, straight into the crowd.

73

'Get his costume off,' shouted one of the more alert onlookers, a man in a bright yellow shirt.

'No! You'll spoil the magic for the children.' His wife gave his arm a slap.

'But he'll suffocate!' The man wrestled with Tigger's head. 'I think that might ruin the magic for them too.'

And when Tigger's head came off to reveal a red-faced teenage girl, yelling, 'No, Mom. I don't want to get up yet!' Janey turned to her mum.

'Mum, I'm really tired. Shall we go now?'

To her relief, her mum nodded. 'I need a dip.'

Ronnie whacked the air conditioning on full and cruised along to the Villas where they'd planned on gathering up the others. It was not as easy as planned. Every one of Janey's spy team was flat out and snoring by the pool. They hadn't moved since that morning. Janey shook Mrs Halliday.

'Mrs H,' she said. 'We're going for a swim in the sea. Do you want to come?'

Mrs Halliday sat up blearily. 'Sharks!' she shouted, then lay down again.

Janey tried Alfie instead. 'Come on, Al. You can try the surf. Let's go.'

'Five minutes,' he groaned, holding up three fingers. Only Leaf responded quickly. 'What is the problem?' He sat up with a start and Janey explained that they were off for a swim in the ocean. 'Ah yes. That is a good idea. I will help you wake the others.' And with that he ran up to the small diving board and launched himself into the pool.

'Whazzat?' G-Mamma sat bolt upright, one of her false eyelashes stuck to her cheek. She patted her damp legs. 'Whysitallwet? Whatsssgoingon? Stopitlittlegreenboy.'

Leaf grinned and dive-bombed the pool again. Within a few moments the resulting splash had roused everybody. 'Come on, you lot,' pleaded Janey. 'A swim will wake you up.'

Alfie groaned, but he still gathered up his surf-board and headed for the car.

The others followed reluctantly, after taking quick Wowers to get into their Spysuit surf gear. Ronnie held the boot open casually, so that Trouble could jump in, and soon they were speeding along towards the coast, the air conditioning raising their spirits as it lowered their temperatures.

The beach looked stunning in the glorious sunlight, as though a sunbeam had been captured and stretched along the coast. Janey pulled her Perspire down over her eyes. All around them, the sand was littered with sleeping bodies in varying shades of sunburn; the spies and Mrs Brown piled their clothes under a sun umbrella and plunged into the sea.

'Do those sunbathers know something we don't?' Tish looked around as they ploughed through the waves. They were the only ones in the water.

Janey glanced back towards the beach. There was only one upright figure – a little boy, watching them solemnly with his arms wrapped around his knees. Behind him, Ronnie leaned on the car, fanning himself and occasionally scratching Trouble's head. 'I think they're all just asleep. Come on, we'll be fine.'

For half an hour they splashed and played in the surf, the adults bobbing in cool bliss, the spylets body-surfing and dunking each other, gradually getting deeper and deeper and allowing the cool water to wake them up thoroughly.

This is fun, thought Janey. Just like a real, normal holiday, doing real things with normal people – well, normalish people. And she allowed herself to cast off the mantle of spylet, and concentrate on being a girl; a girl, playing with her friends in the churning, foaming sea, having a great holiday.

The only thing was, the sea was splashing and churning for a particular reason.

They were not alone.

Chapter 10 Supersize snacks

Jean Brown was floating on her back, eyes closed and completely relaxed when a jet of water shot up out of the ocean, a few meres behind her. Janey caught sight of the little fountain, and then she saw another. And another. All around them, getting ever closer, was a circle of water jets.

Janey's heart thudded as she caught sight of something else glistening, moving fast just under the surface of the water.

'Er, Mum,' she said quietly. '*Everyone*. I think you should head towards me. Slowly. Don't splash.'

Jean Brown's instant response was to thrash over onto her front and kick towards Janey. 'What? What is it?'

Janey's heart sank. Only a short distance behind her mum, the water parted for a second and a slick sliver of whale-skin bobbed into view, then disappeared. The whale was closer than it had been before.

The others, responding to the warning tone in Janey's voice, had fallen silent. G-Mamma pulled on her goggles – Ultra-gogs, thought Janey – and did a neat and splashless tuck-and-dive beneath the surface. She popped up again a moment later, much closer to Janey.

'Fishy fiascos!' she squeaked. 'Killer whales!'

'No one thrash!' hissed Janey. 'Keep calm.'

The spout of water behind Mrs Brown was now so close that it actually looked to Janey as though it were coming out of the top of her mum's head. The whale could be just about to open its death-rimmed jaws and snap her up. Hardly thinking what she was doing, and ignoring her own advice, Janey hauled herself out of the water and onto her ASPIC. Just as she cruised to her mother's side, the terrifying mouth reared out of the water, open, ready to strike. 'Janeeeeyy!' screeched Jean Brown.

In one movement, Janey bent down to scoop her mother up on to the front of ASPIC, and extended one leg behind her. The killer whale's teeth grazed the bare skin below her golden Spysuit as she lifted her foot and banged hard against the whale's tongue. Her Four F's exploded, with a dual effect: firstly, she and her mother shot off across the ocean, her mum straddling the board and hanging on wildly with both arms, Janey balanced on one leg like a crazed ballerina; secondly, the whale got a very nasty and with a low trumpeting sound it snapped its jaws together and dived under the water.

Janey's ASPIC collided with Alfie. He and Leaf were back-to-back on their boards, Alfie covering for Leaf as he punched questions into his Perspire as quickly as his water-sodden fingers would allow. 'Come on,' muttered Alfie. 'We're completely surrounded. Find out what we can do!'

'I am trying. This is madness. This should not be happening,' said Leaf, glancing up anxiously.

Meanwhile Tish, G-Mamma and Mrs Halliday were all lined up on Tish's board, standing in a row and not daring to put a toe into the water as the circling water spouts got nearer and nearer, and ominous flashes of whale-skin broke the surface.

'How many are there?' Janey pulled her mum to her feet and got her balance on the board. 'Two? Three?'

Alfie turned to her, his face grim. 'Eleven. There are eleven of them. And six of us.'

Janey put her arms around her mum's waist. For the rest of them it was terrifying, but for Jean Brown this was plain madness. All she knew was that a group of killer whales had surrounded a random group of swimmers, and were about to eat them up. She squeezed Janey hard and dropped a kiss on her forehead. 'I haven't protected you. That's my job, as your mother, and I've failed you.'

'No, you haven't,' said Janey fiercely. 'You're brilliant. You don't know how brilliant …'

'That's why everyone stayed on the beach,' said Jean quietly. 'I'm so sorry, Janey.'

Janey shook her head, gasping as water spouted up from the ocean, just metres away. She glanced at the sleeping figures on the beach– and her breath caught in her throat. The eleven water spouts were grouped in a neat circle, all around them, but she wasn't looking at them. Instead, her eyes fixed on one of the only figures on the beach that wasn't asleep.

Trouble.

Right at that moment, all the jets of water died away. Janey sensed that the killer whales were waiting for something: a signal to attack 'Trouble!' she screamed.

'Come here, Twubs! Everyone, get closer to me and Mum.'

The spy team leapt into action, paddling, ASPICing, dragging their way across the choppy water towards Janey, just as eleven sets of teeth rose out of the ocean. The whales were ready to strike the moment they were instructed to do so.

Janey looked around. And there it was – a hideous tentacle rising momentarily out of the water and slapping the surface like a conductor striking his podium with his baton. Copernicus.

She looked left. The water around them was bubbling, alive with the motion of eleven enormous bodies – twelve, now she knew the hideous squid-man was there too. But help was on the way.

Trouble was sleek and glorious, his golden tail streaming out behind him and his quiff flattened by the wind as he scooted across the ocean on what looked like his own tiny surfboard. Then, with an enormous yowl of satisfaction, Trouble launched himself off his board, sank his claws into one of the whales enormous whales, and raced up the slope of its back, jumping neatly over the spout-hole and springing in a graceful somersault right off the tip of the its nose …

… and straight into Janey's arms. 'Hang on everyone!' she yelled.

Then she grabbed the little glass bell that the spy-cat always wore around his neck. The bell that was actually a

Spyroscope, an amazing spy-buy that activated a powerful and dangerous vortex that protected only those at its centre.

The effect was as dramatic and the Spyroscope sprang into action. Suddenly the spy team were lifted above the ocean in a bubble of air, while all around them chaos reigned. The whales were thrashed about, unable to stop themselves from being tossed around by the awesome power of the Spyroscope. Janey whooped with joy as whale after whale flipped helplessly and sailed through the air, landing far, far away.

Then she saw the mutated, disfigured form of Copernicus, screeching with rage and flying through the sky, tossed up out of the ocean by Trouble's spy-buy, tentacles twisting and thrashing helplessly. 'How … what …' Jean Brown stared at Janey and then back at the pandemonium outside the vortex.

Janey thought quickly. 'IMAX!' she said. 'We're in the…er…land of theme parks, remember. It's all a, um, *3D Experience*. Nothing to worry about at all.'

Her mother frowned and then sighed. 'Well, honestly. That was much too life-like for my liking. And what's that – the parting of the Red Sea?'

They all followed her gaze, and Janey smothered a grin. The Spyroscope had created a tunnel between two walls of water. The tunnel reached almost as far as the beach.

'Wow. What an effect!' Janey smiled at her mum, and moments later they were all running for the safety of the shore.

As soon as they were in the shallows, Janey let go of the Spyroscope. They waded knee-deep through the water to the beach, while behind them the twin cliffs of sea-water wobbled and wavered, then collapsed in on themselves, millions of gallons of water crashing together in a maelstrom of sand and ocean and some rather large sea creatures.

Safely out of the water, they collapsed in a line along the sand.

'They really should warn you when they're going to pull that kind of stunt,' said Janey's mum, staring out at the ocean.

Mrs Halliday sat up and looked around. 'There's your proof that it's just another display, Jean,' she said, pointing down the beach. 'Nobody even bothered to wake up for it.'

Janey looked at the sunbathers. It was true. Nobody had even stirred from their sleep.

'Weird,' said Alfie.

But one person was awake, and he was watching them now with solemn, dark eyes. It was a little boy, all alone, clutching his knees to his chest and scratching his head occasionally.

Janey leaned across to G-Mamma. 'He might need brain-wiping.'

'Okay, Blondalicious, I'll check him out.'

82

G-Mamma hauled herself to her feet and trotted over to the boy. 'Hello! We're going to get an ice-cream. Want one?'

The boy shook his head.

'Candy? Doughnuts?'

Again the boy shook his head.

'Well,' said G-Mamma, perplexed – she'd just offered him all her favourite things and he'd refused – 'Is there anything you would like?'

And at that, the boy picked up a stick and drew in the sand. Janey now approached and looked closely at the drawing. It was a little circle on top of a big circle, with two tiny circles on either side of the bigger circle. 'Potatoes?' she asked helplessly.

The boy shook his head again, sadly.

'What's your name?' said Janey.

He picked up the stick again and wrote the number 12.

'No,' said Janey. 'Your name. Like my name is Janey.'

The little boy shrugged, picked up his stick again, and pointed at the number 12.

'Well, if you get hungry, just come and ask,' said G-Mamma, grabbing Janey's arm and walking away. 'No need to brain-wipe,' she whispered. 'He's not going to tell anyone.'

'How do you know?'

'Because I don't think he can speak,' said G-Mamma.

Janey felt so sorry for the little boy that she wanted to turn straight back to him. He seemed so sad and lonely. But the rest of their party was at the umbrella, gathering their things together, and now that the sun had sunk a little and the temperature had dropped, the other sunbathers were beginning to stir. Then when she looked to see whether the boy needed her help, he had disappeared. He must have left with his family, she thought. Well I'm sure they'll look after him.

They clambered into the huge car again to make their way back to the Villas, a much more subdued party than the one that had been splashing in the sea just hours before. Janey turned to Alfie. 'How many whales did you say there were?'

Leaf spoke for him. 'Eleven! Eleven killer whales!' He sounded incredibly angry – and with good reason, thought Janey. Copernicus had just tried to wipe them all out in one go.

Janey turned and stared out of the window. Her Blonde instincts were turning over and over in her stomach, warning her that she had missed something important. Something obvious . . .It wasn't simply that Copernicus had tried to kill them all. There was something else.

She couldn't work it out now. But Jane Blonde was determined to get to the bottom of it. Soon.

Chapter 11 Revolution

While Jean went for a lie-down, Janey and the team gave Abe a full debrief. He peered anxiously into the camera and his face loomed up on the Spylab's plasma screen. 'Did Jean buy the '3D experience' story,' he asked. .

G-Mamma sniffed. 'That woman believes anything these days. Apart from the truth. Can't we just tell …'

'No,' said Abe, defiantly. 'It's not the right time. She can know all about us when she needs to. You have to remember what a shock it will be to her. Especially finding out her daughter is Jane Blonde.'

Janey could only begin to imagine what state that particular bit of information would get Jean Brown into.

She listened respectfully as the others shared their concerns with Abe. 'Nothing goes to plan,' said Leaf with a sigh.

Abe shook his head. 'So it seems. I'm sorry you all had to go through that.'

'Eleven killer whales!' said Leaf, angrily.

'Ahhh, there's song in that!' G-Mamma beamed. 'Eleven Killer Wha-ales, Ten Hungry Hippos, Nine naughty nippers, Eight Angry 'Gators, Something something something …Five … Gold … Rings …'

But Jancy didn't hear much after 'Ten Hungry Hippos.' There hadn't been ten hippos. There had been eleven. Eleven whales, and eleven hippos. And there was something else …

Janey now spoke out loud. 'They weren't regular killer whales. They weren't black and white – they were *grey* and white. And they were far smaller than regular killer whales. Just like Helios was at Seaworld…'

'What are you getting at Blonde?' asked Alfie.

'Yes, tell us Janey. What's on your mind?' Her father's eyes seemed to glitter with anticipation. Janey took a deep breath.

'The whales…I think they *were* hippos. Something's been done to them. They've been sort of altered.'

As she spoke, Abe seemed to stagger backwards and slump into a chair, his mouth open and his face grey.

'He knows,' was all he said.

'Dad? What does he know?'   Abe shook his head. 'He knows about Revolution. He's got ahead of me.' He fumbled around with something, and then said, 'Wait for me there.'

Janey's heart jumped. Her father was coming! On the one hand that filled her with joy, but on the other it made her very nervous – if her father was coming out of hiding, he was seriously worried.

Moments later Abe materialised next to the open French doors, various cells and body parts joining up like a complex 3D jigsaw, before their very eyes. As soon as he had reformed, he locked the French doors behind him and strode across to his team. He touched Janey's arm briefly before he turned to the others.

'I have to tell you this in person. It's the most awe-inspiring, and potentially most monstrous discovery I've ever made.

Janey thought about the people looking after him at Solfari Lands – Ivan Erikssen, Magenta, and the Bird family. Blackbird had already betrayed him once. Abe was right to mistrust her, to get out of the way and deliver the information to them direct.

Abe stared at his feet for a moment, then sighed. 'Revolution. I sometimes wish these things never occurred to me. They seem to get the world into trouble.'

'Revolution is like … war, isn't it, sir?' said Alfie. He, his mother and G-Mamma moved instinctively together, closing ranks, preparing for battle.

'Yes. No. Not like you think.' Abe paced distractedly. 'This particular revolution is a little different.'

With that he took a laser pen from his pocket, projected it onto the ceiling, and wrote 'R Evolution' in large red letters. After a few moments the image faded, and the spies looked back at their leader, puzzled.

'Not Revolution. It's R-Evolution. That's what this process is. Rapid Evolution. Using this methodology – which is a long way from perfected, I should add – we can take a creature in one form and speed up the way it evolves.'

'You make it grow up fast?' said Tish, saying out loud what everyone else was thinking.

Abe shrugged. 'In a manner of speaking. You make it *change* very quickly. In less than an hour, we can make a creature evolve into what it would be now from what it probably was millions of years ago.'

There was silence while everyone worked out what this meant, then Alfie said, 'So you mean that, in theory, you could take a sabre-tooth tiger and turn it into a regular tiger?' Abe nodded gravely.

G-Mamma yelped. 'Or a mammoth into an elephant?'

'Yes.'

Now Janey spoke. 'And a hippo?'

Her father sighed. 'Most people don't realise this, but the hippo's closest relative is not the horse that it was named after. It's the whale. That's what their forebears might have evolved into.'

'So Copernicus has found out about R-Evolution, stolen some hippos, and changed them into killer whales?' Janey gulped. This was bad news, on so many levels. Not only did it mean that a double agent was passing information onto Copernicus; it also meant that Copernicus had yet another means of creating armies of killer creatures …

Abe strode around the room, thinking aloud. 'So. We have to track down Copernicus and stop him. I'm sure stealing a few hippos is just the beginning.'

88

'Sir, could the process be reversed? Like could you make … *dinosaurs*?'

Again, Abe could only nod, but his eyes were filled with horror. After a moment's silence he managed to recover himself. He spoke quickly.

'Alfie, you and your mum, and Leaf, track down Copernicus for me.' He resumed his circuit of the lab. 'Tish, G-Mamma, you can come back with me. I'm going to close down the Solfari Lands Spylab. In fact, I'm stopping all R-Evolution research. It's too dangerous. I want you for extra security if anything turns nasty. And Tish, you can come back and see your mother.'

'What about me?' asked Janey, sure that she'd have a key part to play in the next phase of the mission. But the bleak expression on her father's face worried her.

'Get your mother home,' he said. 'Make sure you're both safe, and then wait for instructions from G-Mamma. *Please, Janey.*'

He said this even before Janey had started to argue, and though she longed to plead with him to let her stay in Florida and help track down Copernicus, she couldn't find the words. The most important thing to Abe was knowing that his family were safe. So Janey simply held his hand for a moment, then nodded.

It was time to part. Her father flung open the balcony doors and zoomed off by SATISPI, closely followed by G-Mamma and Titian Ambition. Leaf and Alfie were already involved in a hot debate about where they should start looking for Copernicus.

'He must have a Spylab in the Everglades,' Alfie was saying.

'We should go to the ocean.' Leaf crossed his arms belligerently. 'That is where we saw him last.'

'Right,' said Alfie, 'so we go to the ocean, in the middle of the night, in the pitch black, with at least eleven killer whales … what am I not liking about this?'

'You are scared, I think.'

'No, not scared,' said Alfie slowly, as if he were talking to an idiot. 'Wise. Sensible. Not keen to be whale food.'

'Boys!' snapped Mrs Halliday in her best head-teacher voice. 'Let's argue about this later. First of all we need to get Janey and Jean back home, safe and sound, and that means you and I, Alfie, will have to go too to avoid suspicion. We'll zap back as quickly as possible. Go and wake your mum up, Janey. It will be dawn soon.'

Janey nodded. Dawn. A new day. She wondered how she would explain to her mum that they had to leave suddenly, but miraculously a plane would be laid on just for them, and all their transport home would be completely organized. 'Why can't I just tell her the truth?' she grumbled as she vaulted through the French doors into her own bedroom. Her dad had made it sound like one day it would be possible. But when?

The sun was just peeking through the blinds as Janey pushed open her mum's door. 'Are you awake?' she said softly.

But then she pushed open the door fully, and her knees gave way.

Her mum wasn't there. The bedside table was overturned and the bedclothes were tangled across the floor as though someone had dragged her mother from her bed, but that wasn't the worst thing.

Janey looked in horror at the black, tar-like writing, plastered graffiti-like across the far wall, splattered over the glass door, her mum's dressing gown on its hook – everywhere. And the message said:

Stay away blonde...

or mummy will stay away. Forever.

Chapter 12 Sky's the limit

Once Janey had calmed down enough to tell Mrs Halliday, Alfie and Leaf what had happened, there was more arguing over where they should head to first.

'He must have taken her to the ocean,' said Leaf. 'It is the most obvious place.'

Alfie curled his lip. 'He won't have a Spylab under the ocean, duh. Way too difficult to build.'

Leaf looked at Alfie smugly. 'He might have her in a submarine, or on a boat.'

'Please Leaf, Alfie,' she said desperately. 'I can't sit here arguing.' Janey was so tired of keeping secrets from her mum that she had sworn to herself that she would tell her everything if – no WHEN – she found her.   'Blonde is right,' said Mrs Halliday, jumping to her feet. 'Alfie, since you're so sure he must be in the Everglades, you go there. Janey, you go with him. Leaf, you and I will go and check out the ocean site we were at earlier.'

The boys knew better than to argue with such authority, and within minutes they had SATISPIed to their respective destinations. Janey's heart bumped around in the bottom of her chest. It didn't matter whether her mum was trapped in the Everglades, or under the ocean: in either place, she would be frightened, and lonely, and worried for Janey. She had to be found.

Once they had rematerialised by the river, Alfie's eyes lit up. 'Allow me,' he said, leaping onto the swamp-buggy and revving the engine loudly. 'Just make it quick,' was all Janey said as she braced herself for the ride.

And quick it was, with Janey nearly finding herself flung off into alligator-infested waters as Alfie careered across the water, tracking his progress in his Ultra-gogs and shouting out landmarks to assure Janey he knew where he was going. 'Duck under these branches, that's right. Yep, tree shaped like an ice-cream cornet – nearly there. Last bend, hold on.'

Suddenly they were at the spot at which Janey had found the hippos. She leapt onto the slippery bank, little caring whether any alligators had spotted her. Then she signalled to Alfie, shoved a SPIder in her mouth, and plunged into the water.

The Ultra-gogs adjusted immediately, giving her relatively clear vision through the gloom of the water. There were a couple of alligators nearby, but they didn't seem at all interested in her. Janey flicked out the titanium blade from the finger of her Girl-Gauntlet, just in case, and went deeper. There was no sign of a Spylab, and Janey's spy instincts told her that her mum wasn't anywhere near. She touched a foot to the river bed to turn around and head back to Alfie, and just then noticed something twinkling in the mud as a shaft of sunlight penetrated the water. Something that looked out of place on the sludgy riverbed.

Janey dug it out with her titanium blade and swam up to the surface.

Wiping it clean with her Gauntlet, Janey inspected her find. It was a mirror, a tiny round mirror on the end of a stick, rather like a lollipop. She waded quickly over to the swamp buggy and clambered aboard.

'Alfie, I found … Alfie!'

Her spylet friend was fast asleep, slumped across the rudder. So much for looking out for her. When Janey shook him he lifted his head and peered at her with one eye. 'S'ot.'

'What?'

'It's hot,' he said more clearly, stretching his arms. 'Find anything?'

Janey showed him the little mirror. 'Only this. Could be a clue though?'

'It looks like one of those things a dentist would use.' Alfie turned the mirror this way and that, looking for marks of some kind. 'Agh!' he cried.

Suddenly a shaft of sunlight bounced off the mirror straight into Alfie's eyes. He twitched it out of the way, and Janey watched, fascinated, as the beam of light headed straight back up the river behind them. If anyone had been at the picnic site, they would have seen the light instantly.

'It's to signal with,' said Janey excitedly. Angling the mirror carefully, she managed to direct the sunlight up against a tree, then straight into the eye of an over-curious alligator who very quickly sank out of sight.

Whipping off her PERSPIRE, she tapped in 'signal mirror' and waited for the information to pop up in the peak of the cap. 'Here we are. Safety mirrors for outdoor pursuits. Well, this is certainly outdoors. That must be it.'

'Or,' said Alfie, peeking over her shoulder, 'maybe it's something to do with that.'

He pointed to the article at the bottom of the page. AN ASTRONAUT'S SURVIVAL KIT, it said, CONSISTS OF A PARACHUTE, INFLATABLE BOAT, TWO DAYS DRINKING WATER, SIGNAL MIRROR …

Janey head spun. Alfie was right. 'That's it,' she said solemnly.. 'Copernicus had that rocket, didn't he?' He'd been trying to escape Antarctica in it last time they had been pitted against each other. . 'But where would he be keeping a rocket rocket? Not under the ocean…'

Then suddenly it came to her, and dread filled Janey's stomach. In her mind's eye she travelled back to the day she had been flicking through her mum's brochures for Florida tourist attractions. And, at once, it all made perfect, horrible, sense.

The Everglades, the ocean, the hippos, the killer whales – they weren't as important as what was built on a small island just off the Florida coast . . .   'I know where he is,' she said to Alfie. 'I know where his lab is and where he's got Mum.'

Alfie spun the swamp buggy around without a second's hesitation, and in seconds they were back at the picnic site, ready to SATISPI.

'Where are we headed?' Alfie waited to tap in the coordinates for their safe landing.

Janey consulted her Ultra-Gogs once more. It had to be right. 'The Space Centre,' she said. 'Cape Canaveral.'

'Oh, my life,' groaned Alfie as he threw her the remote and disintegrated into a steady stream of cells, flowing skywards.

Copernicus wanted to reach the stars, thought Janey. But she was going to stop him.

Chapter 12 Cape capers

To Janey's horror, she materialised directly in front of a large crowd of awe-struck school-children. 'Alfie,' she hissed, frantically looking around.

'And … err … don't miss the show later,' she heard him say. 'Holograph spectacular, 1pm.'

Alfie was standing just behind her. Janey took the hint and waved at the children, half of whom already looked bored – or just plain tired - and were wandering off to the next exhibit.

Alfie picked up a visitor's guide that one of the children had dropped. The child was now propped in a nearby seat, enjoying a morning nap.

'What is wrong with everyone?' said Janey, staring at the child and then at the map. 'So we're in the Visitor Complex of the Spacer Center. Where would The Big C be hiding?'

Alfie had retreated into a bush and was busy SPIVing his mum, so Janey studied the leaflet. There was a garden to the left of them, with a collection of grounded rockets, and behind that a curious dome that looked like a possible Spy lab location. To the right there was a black spherical structure, that appeared to be floating on its own little lake. Copernicus had a passion for black, and Janey decided to check it out first.

Mrs Halliday and Leaf SATISPIed discreetly behind some trees at the back of the Rocket Garden and ran over,

Alfie in tow. 'Where would he have put your mother, Janey?' said Mrs Halliday, laying a hand on Janey's shoulder.

Janey felt a rush of warmth for the matter-of-fact SPI. No matter how dangerous the plans of the mad Copernicus might be, Agent Halo knew that nothing was as important to Janey as finding her mum. 'I was wondering about this black ball thing.'

'I am thinking he would like the dome,' said Leaf, pointing to the left.

'Well, let's split up.' Janey pointed over to the black sphere. 'We'll go that way,' she said, nodding to Alfie, 'and Halo and Leaf can check out the dome.'

'Why don't you come with me?' asked Leaf, but Janey and Alfie were already picking their way through the crowds. Janey reached the sphere several paces before Alfie. She turned and waited for him to catch up, and he staggered to her side. 'Don't know what's the matter with me,' he said, panting. 'This weather's just too much.'

'It doesn't matter,' said Janey. 'This can't be it anyway.'

They both looked at the black sphere. There were small children hanging off the orb, trying to push it around its little lake. Their teacher had given up, and was barely responded when one of the children prodded him in the thigh.

'It's too busy,' said Janey. 'He wouldn't risk being this open, particularly in his current freaky state.'

Suddenly her SPIV bounced against her chest, and she peered at it to see Leaf's thin, upside-down face. 'Blonde,' he whispered. 'We've found a Spylab entry tubes. This must be it.'

There was a bit of confusion on the tiny screen and then Mrs Halliday's face appeared. 'I'm not so sure, Leaf.'

'But I think Blonde should come and check it out …'

'No,' said Janey quietly. 'I've worked it out, I think. Come over to Space Shuttle Plaza.'

She showed Alfie the map as she started to jog over to the Plaza. 'Look, there's a space shuttle there that you can actually go on, and a lake next to it.'

'Alfie nodded. 'Could be it. Look, you … ow, I've got a stitch … you run on ahead. I'll catch you up.'

'Come on, Alfie,' she said, , linking her arm through his so she could half-drag him along as she ran. It wasn't too difficult to make progress, despite the crowds and the extra weight of Alfie Most visitors seemed to be flaking out on the grassy verges, taking forty winks, or walking along sluggishly. In a matter of minutes she had made her way to Space Shuttle Plaza. 'Look, Alfie,' she said, staring in awe at the shuttle. A real rocket, and anyone could go inside.

Alfie's head lolled back 'Awesome,' he yawned.

'This is it, I can just feel it. And … yes!' Janey let Alfie slide to the ground and ran around the shuttle. There, beside the water, was a tar-like slick e – revolting squid-ink, secreted by Copernicus as he hauled himself out of the water and into his lab.

She moved closer to the pool. It made more sense for the lab to be closer to the lake than the shuttle itself, as most people would be interested in the shuttle itself. Although that wasn't the case today, thought Janey. Few people seemed to have the strength to climb the steps to the shuttle door, in fact there was hardly anyone around apart from Alfie, who was leaning against a bin with his head in his hands. Leaf and Mrs Halliday were coming up behind him, both moving slowly, Leaf apparently propping up Agent Halo in the same way Janey had had to support Alfie.

And then she saw it, winking next to the pool. A tiny disc. Excited, Janey pressed it, but nothing happened. She pressed again, waving to the others to join her, but still nothing happened.

'Mi …mirror,' panted Alfie, his hands on his knees and his hair dark with sweat.

'Of course!' Janey fished out the signal mirror from the Everglades and held it at different angles until a shaft of light shot from the signal mirror and connected with the silver disc on the ground. Like ripples on a pond, the light flooded outwards, and Janey found herself staring straight down a wide tube leading directly, she was sure, into one of Copernicus's Spylabs.

'I'll go first,' she said, then stopped short.

It appeared she wasn't just going to go first. She was going alone. Mrs Halliday had joined Alfie next to the bin and was fast asleep. Leaf had curled up on the grass and was also close to sleep.

Janey looked around. Every single person was asleep apart from, Janey realised, a woman in a yellow sundress, who was chucking water from a bottle over her boyfriend, trying to stir him into action

There was no waking Alfie or Mrs Halliday, but Leaf came to when Janey poked at him with her foot. 'Come on. I've got to rescue my mum. And then we'll see what's wrong with everyone.'

'Yes, yes,' he said, brushing grass off his Spysuit, so that Janey just caught a glimpse of gold beneath the green of his cuff. 'I am coming now, Blonde.'

One by one they jumped down the entry tube into the lab. It looked exactly as Janey had expected – shimmering, black, lit only by a few holes in the ceiling. The only thing that wasn't black were their two spysuits, and a glint of white behind a bench. A blouse. A once-neat-but-now-dishevelled white blouse.

'Mum!'

Janey ran over in an instant. Her mum was bound to a chair with some kind of cable, and her head jerked forward at the sound of Janey's voice. 'Darling! Oh, you shouldn't have come here.'

'I've come to rescue you.' Janey flicked out her titanium blade and sawed through the cable.

'But the Squid Man ...' whispered her mother. 'He'll be back any minute, and he's been talking about you, saying all these ridiculous things about you being a ... a *spylet*? Whatever that is. Apparently you keep spoiling his plans and now he's going to spoil *your* plans. Don't let him find us here!'

'I won't, Mum. Can you stand up?' She helped her mother to her feet.

Jean Brown swayed alarmingly. 'I'm so sleepy. His light . . . it makes me so sleepy. And that noise ...'

'What noise?'

Janey leaned into the silence and suddenly heard a very strange sound, a kind of hysterical chattering.

Janey draped her mum's arm over her shoulder. 'Come on. I'll get you out of here. There's all sorts of strange stuff I need to tell you, but I promise I'll explain everything to you, just as soon as I can.'

'Okay,' said Mrs Brown meekly. The strain of her kidnapping seemed to have taken all the fight out of her. Or maybe it was the heat, which seemed to have extracted the fizz from just about everybody.

Janey looked around for the remote control for a SATISPI remote control. It would be the quickest and easiest way to get her mum to safety.

Leaf had already found it. 'Great,' said Janey. 'I'll send my mum first, maybe to Dad at Solfari Lands. Then if you help me get the Halos downstairs I'll send them, and then you, and I'll go last.'

But Leaf wasn't responding. Instead he was staring over Janey's shoulder, an anxious expression on his face, and Janey could just *feel* what –who – must be standing behind her.

The tall figure of Copernicus stood between her and the entry tube. By his side was someone Janey had almost forgotten about – the little boy from the beach, who had been watching them so seriously, and had written his name in the sand: Twelve.

'Right,' said Janey. 'No wonder he doesn't have a name if he's just one of your spylets. He's a bit young though, isn't he?'

Copernicus exhaled - a long, slow expulsion of air that seemed to fill the lab with evil - and the strange chattering, laughing sound from beyond the lab grew louder. 'Blonde. Blonde, Blonde. You have managed to cause me enough trouble despite your tender years. How young is too young?' He laughed bitterly. 'Actually he's even younger than you think.'

Janey tried to flick her eyes towards Leaf. If they could get to the entry tubes somehow, the SATISPI could at least zap her mother out of here. But Leaf appeared to be transfixed, entranced by Copernicus. She was on her own. 'Well, if you'll just excuse me,' she said, trying for an almighty bluff, 'I've just got to get my mum home. By the way, your son's up there.' And she nodded up the tube, hoping to distract her enemy.

But Copernicus rounded on her like a viper. 'Your mother goes nowhere. At least, not with you. She can come with me when I take off, very, very shortly. Didn't I tell you? Stay away. Or Mummy stays away …'

'Forever,' finished Leaf. He looked helplessly at Janey.

So that was it. They were trapped. Alfie and Mrs Halliday had been sedated or something. Leaf had been frozen into inactivity by the close presence of evil incarnate. Janey herself was hampered by her mother's weight as Jean Brown tried, and failed, to regain the use of her legs. The only person who seemed alert was the little boy – Twelve – whose head tilted longingly in the direction of the jabbering laughter.

And Janey suddenly realised something. Twelve was distracted. Maybe he wasn't a tiny spylet at all – he was far too interested in what was going on beyond the laboratory walls. Just like a normal little boy would be.

Which meant that, if her instincts were right, he wouldn't try to stop her if she made it to the entry tube.

And with a quiet, 'Sorry, Mum,' in her mother's ear, she thrust her mum across the lab towards Copernicus. To her immense relief, , she discovered she had made the right assumption about Copernicus. He was simply a Retro-Spectre - a holographic image made up from memories of what he used to be like, before Jane Blonde had given him tentacles.

Jean Brown fell to the floor and slid straight through the wispy body of Copernicus. In seconds she was under the entry tube. In the same short moment, Janey flew across to Leaf, grabbed the remote from his hand and SATISPIed her bewildered mother into space, hopefully back to the safety of Solfari Lands.

Then she pocketed the control, grabbed Leaf by the arm and made a break for the outside. For sunshine. For safety.

Chapter 14 Countdown

Janey and Leaf bounced out of the entry tube and landed just in front of Alfie and Mrs Halliday. 'Alfie! Halo. Al Halo.' Janey hissed in each of their faces, but they merely blinked. 'Oh, this is hopeless!'

Leaf, at least, seemed to have composed himself.. 'So what now?'

'Copernicus is stealing a rocket. This place isn't just for tourists – rocket's really take off from here, and he's going to steal one. Let's get over to Mission Control. I think he's planning to launch soon.'

A quick glance at the information leaflet informed her that the Launch Control Centre was over to their right. In normal circumstances it would have required a long walk. But these were not normal circumstances. 'Everyone's so dozy they won't notice us Fleet-Footing,' said Janey decisively. 'Come on.'

Leaf only hesitated for a second, irritation flashing briefly across his face. Like Alfie, thought Janey, he doesn't like being upstaged by a girl. 'Okay. I come too,' said the green-suited spylet, and he sprinted off across the grass in the direction of the Launch Centre.

Only the woman in the dress, who had given up trying to revive her boyfriend and was now eating his way through their picnic bag, had the energy to say, 'What the …' as they sped by, and only moments later they were approaching the Launch Centre. The pale concrete building glowed ominously in the brilliant sunshine,.

Leaf jolted to a halt at Janey's side. 'Copernicus has probably gone in from underneath,' she said. 'We'll have to be careful.'

Splitting up, they ran around the exterior of the building, but when they found no evidence, they met up again in front of the main door. More out of curiosity than anything, Janey gave it a gentle shove. Despite the obvious entry card system, the door swung open.

They exchanged glances and stepped through. Directly ahead was a large desk which should have been bustling with security guards. Instead there was one weary woman with her chin on the desk.

'This is the Launch Control Centre, isn't it?' Janey looked around uncertainly, and then peeked over the desk. Two security guards were stretched out on the floor next to the woman's chair, snoring roundly.

'Last time I looked,' said the woman with a yawn. 'But in this heat, who the heck cares?'

'But …'

Leaf grabbed Janey's arm. 'Thank you. Then we will just …' and he pointed down the corridor.

'Sure.' The woman nuzzled her head down onto her arms. 'Wake me up on your way back.'

Janey frowned at her then ran quickly after Leaf. Every door swung open at their touch, and every security person, scientist and engineer they passed was either sound asleep or so relaxed that they simply waved to them, rubbing their foreheads and trying to clamp their jaws around yet another yawn.

'This is really weird,' said Janey. Then she gasped.

They had reached a corridor with a huge bank of windows on either side. On one side, she could see a large rocket in the distance. On the other, the two spylets could look down on a room peopled by engineers and labelled with distinctive signs: MAIN PROPULSION SYSTEMS; LIQUID OXYGEN; REACTION CONTROL SYSTEM.

'Mission Control,' said Leaf with a glint in his eye.

It was hugely impressive, and Janey wished that Alfie could see it too – the ultimate in boys' toys. But there was no time to lose, because drifting around the centre of the room, holographic eyes fixed on a screen showing the same large rocket they could see through the windows, was a sinister Retro-Sceptre of Copernicus as he had once been.

'We have to be quick! He's brain-wiped them or something. They're under his control'

Janey chewed quickly on a tiny piece of SPInamite, lodged it onto one of the window frames, and covered her head and Leaf's. There was a small explosion and a rain of glass which caused some of the engineers below to sluggishly lift their heads from the desks and computer keyboards. Now Janey was standing next to a neat hole in the window. As fast as she could, she unwound her SuSPInder and abseiled down into Mission Control. Leaf quickly followed.

Janey ran across to the nearest engineer and shook him by his shoulder. 'That man's stealing a rocket.'

The man blinked blearily at her. furiously. 'He can have it.'

'Have it? It's a rocket!'

Janey couldn't believe what she was hearing. She looked around. All the engineers looked equally relaxed about the fact a strange man was making off with one of their most prized possessions. 'It's a matter of national security,' she yelled. 'International. Global, even!'

'Well … whatever,' said the man with a shrug, and he propped his forehead against his computer monitor and drifted off to sleep.

The Retro-Spectre of Copernicus had barely taken his eyes off the screen. A countdown, in important red numbers, was flashing in the top right-hand corner.

19.30.

'You're completely wasting your time,' said the Retro-Spectre, not even bothering to look at Janey. 'But then, you're good at that, aren't you, Blonde? Wasting Time. Especially … mine!'

Janey didn't care. He could sound as threatening as he liked. He was just a hologram: a ghost, really, and ghosts couldn't hurt her. She had nineteen and a half minutes and she had to make every second count. Running straight through the image of Copernicus, Janey called out to Leaf. 'Flick switches. Press alarm buttons. Do something – anything – that stops that rocket taking off.'

18.40.

But Leaf seemed incapable of doing anything when Copernicus was around, even in Retro-Sceptre form, so Janey had to do everything herself.

17.20.

'It's all pre-programmed,' said the Retro-Spectre. 'And of course, I'm not really here. Do you really think I would be so stupid as to leave something like this to chance?'

16.50

'Something like what?' said Janey helplessly.

The Retro-Spectre turned to her with a vile sneer. 'My planet. My chance to rule the universe. At long last.'

15.55.

'You're mad. You can't rule the universe on your own. And you're not taking Alfie this time,' she said.

15.10.

'No, I won't be taking Alfie. He will be … disposed with.' Copernicus eyed her with something approaching sadness. 'But I will not be alone.'

Janey's heart sank. 'Where's Alfie? How can you kill your own son?'

14.40

'It is regretful,' said Copernicus with a sigh. 'But he has shown where his loyalties lie. I have new off-spring now who will stand by me.'

Janey followed his eyes to the rocket. Cages were being loaded onto it. Cages she had seen before. Filled with … monkeys.

'They're apes,' she said. 'Not people.'

13. 20.

Copernicus simply smiled, and then laughed, the horrible keening sound whistling through Mission Control. 'They are not people. But I think you met my new son.'

And he turned around and pointed to a little boy, all fitted out in a space suit, climbing aboard the rocket.

'Twelve,' said Janey softly.

'Oh, at least. And many more.' Copernicus laughed again. 'I'll have everyone I need with me. And you, Blonde, will be no more.'

11.40.

Janey had no idea what he meant, but at that moment two doors opened opposite each other, and a pair of gorillas pounded along the pathways between the computers towards her.

'Back to the Spylab,' snapped Copernicus as two huge hairy hands grasped her arms, ' and then suited up and on the launch before the lab explosion. I'll be taking the tube. You've only …'

10.01

'… ten minutes,' whispered Janey, slithering helplessly along the tiled floor as the gorillas thrust her through a door and into a deep, barely-lit corridor.

Ten minutes until the rocket took off. Ten minutes before he left the Earth behind. Ten minutes until he blew up the Spylab and everything in it.

As soon as she was flung into the Spylab beneath Space Shuttle Plaza, her heart sank. Alfie and his mother were sitting on the same chair Jean Brown had been strapped to, but were tied up to a sink. Both were still snoring and dribbling.

There was an outraged snarl from the other side of the room, and Janey spun around, expecting to see the gorillas again, but finding instead a furious G-Mamma, cocooned as if by a spider in a length of cable so that only her nostrils, eyes and hair poked out. Beside her lay Tish, mummified in exactly the same way.

Janey ran across and sliced through their bonds with the titanium blade. 'What are you doing here?'

'Me? What are you doing here, Blonde Bombshell?' G-Mamma shimmied her way out of the cable. 'This place is about to blow. I thought at least you'd escape.'

'We tried to get in touch with everyone but nobody was answering,' explained Tish, rubbing her arms vigorously. 'So Abe sent us back. We ran straight into some … well, apes … and they brought us in here.'

'This is bad.' Janey knew just how bad. 'We've got about seven minutes to get out of here.'

The three of them skidded around the room, trying to locate and escape route. Janey tried SPInamiting the closed-over entry tube but could only blow a hole the size of a fist. Copernicus must have had it is specially reinforced. Janey even sent a desperate emails, realising, grimly, that the screensaver showed the soon-to-be-stolen rocket, the countdown (now at 3.20) and the numbers 28.6178N and 80.6125W.

There was no reply.

2.40.

Janey ran to the Hallidays. 'Please wake up! We need to get out of here.'

'They've been sedated,' said Tish, not very helpfully. 'Sound asleep.'

1.50.

'Well, I think it's time for a final rap.' G-Mamma flexed her hands in front of her. 'Ahem...

We're on our way to that Spyland above

But luckily with the people we love

And when we get there we'll find with glee

Who finally gets rid of the evil C.

Let's hear it for the Sol Spies! Whoooooo!'

1.25.

Janey thought of something . . . and almost smiled ....
'G-Mamma, say that again.'

1.10.

With a beam and the glimmer of a tear in her eye, G-Mamma sang out: 'Finally my gift is appreciated!

We're on our way to that Spyland above, but ...'

0.55

'That's it,' said Janey. 'Roll the Halos under the entry tube and join them.'

0.45

'No good, Blonde,' said Tish. 'If you're trying to SATISPI, the remote's missing.'

0.30.

'Oh no it's not,' said Janey, and she pulled it out from the sleeve of her golden Spysuit.

0.20.

She only hoped that the coordinates she was keying in would take her where she thought they would.

10.

' …78N and 80.6125W.'

9.

8

7

6.

5

4

3

'Hang on, everyone!

2

And as the blinking numbers turned to **1**, and the Spylab juddered with a teeth chattering explosion, Janey watched the others disintegrate into streams of cells, and knew that the same thing was happening to her as they SATISPIED out through the atmosphere, through a hole the size of a fist, and chased the rocket that was now hurtling through the skies almost as fast as they were.

But just what, Janey wondered, had happened to Leaf?

Chapter 15 Space race

As Janey had desperately hoped, they materialised together again inside the rocket that Copernicus had stolen and launched.

Once Janey's eyeballs had popped themselves back into their sockets, she found that she was the last to arrive. They were in some sort of baggage hold, except that the baggage wasn't being held. And it was rather unusual baggage.

Her feet, newly re-attached, left the floor, and Janey found herself floating upside down towards the ceiling. Or was it the floor? It was all very hard to tell. G-Mamma, giving her a gleeful thumbs-up, was whipping around in somersaults and bouncing off the cylindrical walls, looking positively graceful and ballerina-like. Tish reached out to try to grab her every now and again, but found it impossible to time her movements correctly, and so she, too, was spinning around the hold in a flurry of red. Alfie, meanwhile, having received a rather rude awakening, was holding onto the back of his mother   And there were other bodies floating around the hold. Wearing an array of bewildered, excited, and downright cross expressions, a dozen or more members of the ape family pirouetted around them, looking completely mystified.

'The poor things!' Janey dropped her voice to a whisper; she didn't want Copernicus to hear them. 'What is he doing with them?'

116

Alfie spun round to face her, and kept going. He slowed himself by grabbing hold of G-Mamma's foot and glared, upside-down, at Janey. 'Never mind what he's doing to them! What are you doing to us? Where are we?'

'Um. On the rocket?' Janey could understand Alfie's confusion. 'You were all tied up in the Spylab, and I got thrown in too, and it was just about to explode, so I used the Space Centre coordinates to follow Copernicus when he launched.'

Alfie looked thunderous for a moment and then suddenly his shoulders dropped. 'Fair enough,' he said gruffly.

Janey took this to mean, 'Well done, good choice, all you could do in the circumstances,' and turned her attention to the gorillas apes that were floating around the hold. 'Let's try and get them under control. Make them hold hands or something,' she said.

G-Mamma lead the way, grabbing hold of a passing chimpanzee. 'Titian, get its other hand. Paw. Thing with fingers.'

As soon as Tish got hold of the other hand, the chimp seemed to relax, and understand what they were doing. It let out a wild chattering which the other chimps, at least, seemed to understand, and another one latched itself onto Tish's free hand and reached for a nearby gorilla. Janey glided around the rocket, orchestrating the hand-holding, and even persuaded Alfie to take his mother's hand in his right one and hold a tiny spider monkey in his left. Before too long the spies, spylets and apes lined the cylindrical hold like a chain of paper dolls, and the chattering subsided to the occasional whimper.

At long last, Janey dared to glance out of the porthole. The earth blinked below them, a tiny sequin of blue and white on the spangled counterpane of the sky. She had seen it from a distance before, courtesy of the SATISPI, but this was tinier, far further away than she had ever known it. Just then the porthole filled up. They were shooting past something … something grey but luminous, with a pitted surface . . .

'Crikey!' squeaked Alfie. 'You know what that is?'

G-Mamma leaned over to the porthole. 'No. Way. Is that … do you think it's made of cheese?'

At that moment Mrs Halliday came to. 'Trust you, Rosie. We appear to be hurtling past the moon and you're thinking about food. I say the more important issue is: *where on earth are we going?*'

'We're not going anywhere on earth,' said Janey. 'He must have finally done it.'

'Done what?' asked Tish .

It was hard to believe. Impossible even. But Copernicus had managed the impossible before, and Janey had long ago realised that he would stop at nothing to meet his bizarre and mind-shattering aims. 'He's always been obsessed with how he should rule the world, the universe even. I overheard him talking in Antarctica. He was trying

118

to steal some of the Earth's core, so that he could Supersize it with his weird machine – and create gravity.'

'Why would he do that?' said Alfie.

Janey heaved a great sigh. 'So he could build his own planet.'

The others stared at her, bobbing up and down. Even the apes seemed to be gazing at her in disbelief. Janey couldn't blame them. It did sound completely mad, but even before she had time to explain herself further, the porthole once again filled with light, and they all turned to look.

'That's the sun,' gasped Tish. 'It's so *golden*.'.

'It can't be the Sun, we'd melt.' Alfie peered out of the glazed panel.

'And we wouldn't be able to look directly at the sun, surely? You can't even do that from the earth,' said Mrs Halliday.

'Frying eyes, you're right!' whooped G-Mamma. ' It's too small to be Sun. So what is it? And … is that me or are we slowing down? Whoa!'

G-Mamma's last shriek was muffled by her skirt falling over her face, as the rocket slowly rotated, and the ring of people and primates found itself upside-down and bouncing around, out of control. Suddenly the chain collapsed in a heap at the bottom of the hold..

'Mum, get your foot out of my nose,' grunted Alfie.

'I can't! I can't move at all.'

119

G-Mamma's faint voice buffeted through from the bottom of the pile. 'You should worry. I've got a manky old monkey bottom on my head ...'

'Shhh!' urged Janey. 'Hide! There's someone coming.'

Footsteps were rattling directly over their head. They had clearly landed, somewhere in space, on the surface of a strange, golden planet. Janey listened hard as she wriggled herself down between an orangutan and a couple of chimps, checking that the other spies were also ducking out of sight. The footsteps above were soft, light – not the step-swish-drag of an enormous squid-like creature. At least it wasn't Copernicus.

As a hatch over their heads slid open, Janey hissed to her Ultra-gogs. 'Periscope,' she said, trying to avoid getting a mouthful of monkey fur.

Success! Instantly, the left lens slid across to cover the right, then a slender crooked tube, like the handle of an umbrella, rose up between the bodies in the hold. Janey had a clear view. She held her breath ...

The figure that appeared over their heads, however, was not in the least bit frightening. Even though she knew that the person in the space-suit, peering down into the hold, was the son and loyal supporter of her arch rival, Janey couldn't help thinking that Twelve looked rather sad behind his helmet.

At once, the chimpanzees started to chatter and surge,. Janey panicked. What if they all moved? They'd be seen!

But to her relief, Twelve shook his head, once, twice, very firmly at a gibbering chimpanzee who was now jumping up and down ecstatically, on what Janey was sure was Alfie's head. He gave the chimp a little wave in one smooth circular movement, put his finger to roughly where his mouth would be beneath the helmet, then held up his hands.

'Zoom!' breathed Janey to her Ultra-gogs, and they focused in on the hands.

She had no idea what the boy was doing. First he held up his left hand and linked his right pinky around his left one. Then he used his right index finger to point at his fourth finger on his left hand. And again. Next, holding out his left palm, he tapped two fingers of his right hand against it. Then he nodded carefully to the chimp and waggled his hand. He's saying 'goodbye' whispered Janey as he slid the hatch door shut.

'Has it gone?' whispered G-Mamma hysterically. 'Because I'm about to suffocate!'

Janey sat up cautiously

and G-Mamma wiggled out between two orangutans, so hot, red and cross that she looked like one of their relatives.

Now Mrs Halliday and the spylets poked up out of the pile of hairy bodies and the apes resumed their restless chattering.

'It was that little boy from the beach,' Janey explained quickly. 'Copernicus says he's his son. His new, *loyal* son.'

'Oh dear,' said Alfie in a flat voice. 'He doesn't need me any more. Tragedy. Boo hoo.'

He stopped abruptly as a fresh barrage of noise filtered down from above. There was a sound like lift doors opening, then a clattering against the side of the rocket, and the SPI team looked swiftly out of the porthole-window.

There were five figures making their way down a ladder, weighted down by their special space boots. The two larger figures were pushing a third, adult-sized person along in front of them. Janey recognized them instantly from the way they hunched over – it was the two gorillas from the Launch Control Centre. The boy called Twelve was out in front, treading in long, laborious steps across to some location that Janey couldn't see. Behind him came a taller figure, slender, more agile. But it was only when the gorillas pushed so hard the adult figure stumbled and turned to berate them, and the slender figure spun round to see what was going on, that Janey was able to work out who they were.

One was someone that Janey had been wondering about. Leaf, his pale features flattened by the screen on his space helmet, was shouting something at the taller person who was trying to get off their knees.

Janey gasped. On a distant planet, way out in who knew where in a far-off galaxy, far, far from home was the last person she expected – or wanted – to see.

'Mum,' she whispered. 'What are you doing here?'

Chapter 15 Japes with apes

Wasn't that—' Alfie started.

'Yes,' said Janey, quietly. 'I've got to follow them.'

Janey looked around for some means of escape. Pointing her Girl-Gauntleted hand at the inner wall of the rocket, she prepared to laser, cut, blast her way out of there – anything to get to her mum as quickly as possible.

'Blondette!' shrieked G-Mamma. 'What are you doing? You cut a hole in this thing and we could all die instantly.'

'Oh.' Janey sat back on her heels, disappointed. 'That's true. We don't even know if it's air out there.'

'Judging by the way Copper Knicker's new son was wearing a space suit, I'm thinking 'no',' said Tish.

The space-suit! That gave Janey an idea. 'I need to get up to the hatch,' she said, pointing above their heads to where Twelve had appeared.

'Your Four-Fs won't get you that far.' Alfie pointed out.

'No,' said Janey, 'but we do have some super strong people launchers.' She looked at the pair of small gorillas and grinned back at Alfie.

'It's a monkey puzzle.' G-Mamma gauged the distance to the hatch. 'How many gorillas does it take to throw a spylet sixty feet?'

'Answer: all of them,' said Janey   The spies and spylets formed the first ring, the base of a tower. On their shoulders the orangutans balanced obligingly. It appeared that nothing was too strange a request for them. Next came the chimpanzees, with the smaller monkeys looped around their arms, strengthening the joints, and finally, after a bit of coaxing and some very strange mimes, Janey persuaded the two young gorillas to scamper up the swaying human-and-ape scaffolding and position themselves at the top.

She'd seen it in Cirque du Soleil. And if ordinary people could do it, surely a spylet with ace gadgetry could manage it? With a deep breath, Janey hauled herself up the tottering tower, slipping slightly when one of the chimpanzees suddenly moved a long arm, and trying to ignore G-Mamma huffing, 'Slowly, slowly, catchy monkey' every few seconds. Finally she reached the top. Hoping beyond all hope that the gorillas understood, and didn't decide to thump her, she gently placed their hands together, and climbed onto the little launch pad they'd created.

The hatch was now twenty feet above her head. Unwinding her SuSPInder from her waist, she looped it over her arm like a lasso, shouted 'Ready! On three,' then showed one, then two, then three fingers to the gorillas. And as her three fingers fell, the gorillas gibbered manically and tossed her into the air. Like a cork from a champagne bottle she shot upwards, unravelling her SuSPInder and throwing it towards the hatch. The first

124

time it fell back down towards her. As quickly as she could, Janey coiled it again and hurled it upwards, The line went taut. The tiny grappling hook had lodged itself in the rim of the hatch; now she just had to haul herself up .

'Erm, problem,' she shouted down to the others. 'There's no handle on this side.'

There was a general muttering from below, then Alfie shouted something.

'*Forget it?* No way Al!'

'No,' he hollered back. '*Four-F* it!'

Ah. Four-F. Good idea. Janey swung upside down as the apes below grunted their approval, then she clamped her feet onto the underside of the metal hatch. She tried not to think about how she was hanging like a bat, sixty feet in the air. With superhuman effort she straightened herself out as much as possible, hanging grimly onto the SuSPInder cord, and pushed up and sideways at the same time.

It had been a *great* idea. The hatch opened just a crack, then a little more as Janey slid her feet to the side. When it was just about wide enough, she popped her feet through the gap so that she was hanging from her knees, then she pulled the rest of her body up. Rather clumsily, she managed to wriggle through the gap until she found herself upright in a small cube of a room. Along one wall was a rail, loaded with space-suits, and to the other side was a small ladder leading to a similar hatch above her head.

Janey found a remote control attached to the wall. She yanked it free and dropped it through the hatch. 'It's an air lock,' she shouted down to her friends. 'I'll have to close this door before I can open the next one. But there's the remote so you can open it that side.' 'Come on, Blonde,' she told herself sternly.

She donned one of the space suits quickly and sped up the ladder, pressing the green button that opened the hatch. 'Wow,' she whistled when she was inside the next segment of the rocket. This was no empty holding area. All around her were flashing lights, tubes and ducts, banks of buttons and dials, tanks, turbos ... Jane Blonde was deep within the operation room of the rocket. This section had seats too, on which the astronauts would be held down in a complex web of straps and buckles. Five seats, counted Janey. A chair for everyone who'd got off. So where had Copernicus been sitting?

There was no time to consider that. He had her mum at his mercy somewhere on his golden planet. She stepped outside, and felt all the air escaping from her body ... not because of a leak in her suit, but because she was actually walking in space. 'Wow,' she said to herself.

The feeling was unlike anything she had ever known before. Excitement, fear, exhilaration – all piled up on top of each other with a headiness that could easily make a person go a little mad. She wanted to throw herself off the ladder ... float out into the galaxy ... feel what it was to be such a miniscule, atom-sized, unimportant part of this amazing, staggering creation …

Just in time, she remembered that someone *had* actually gone mad, *had* tried to be part of the creation process. And more to the point – they were holding her mum hostage. Janey forced herself off the ladder onto the surface of the planet. It felt firm underfoot – just like the Earth, really, though when she moved another foot forward the ground seemed to shimmy just out of reach before she made contact and felt it, firm and steady again.

'Slowly, slowly catchy monkey,' she said with a smile.

She was just about to take her third step when there was a blinding flash in front of her, some thirty or forty metres away. To her astonishment, a tall, deformed figure, his space suit specially adapted to fit his tentacled body, seemed to step out of nothingness.

Janey stopped. There was no tiny rocket beside him; no visible means by which Copernicus could have just arrived on his planet of gold, but he clearly had just appeared. Spotting Janey, he waved two of his tentacles impatiently and slithered away.

Janey allowed herself to breathe out. Thanks to the space-suit, he hadn't recognized her. He must have thought she was someone else, a member of his team. As quickly as she could, Janey lunged across the sandy surface, following him.   When Janey reached the spot where Copernicus had appeared, she couldn't believe her eyes.

'No way,' said Janey. It couldn't be … but it certainly looked like … 'A bus stop?!'

The slender pole waved in the wind, a breeze that appeared to be coming from a shimmering disc of dense air next to it. She peered more closely at the bus stop sign which had something printed on it in large golden letters. 'Copernicus.'

Janey touched the pole gingerly, but nothing happened - although the strange wind that blew from the disc seemed to gust more strongly. Turning her back, Janey stepped off in the direction Copernicus had taken. She could no longer see him which meant that he must be inside somewhere, maybe in a Spylab.

After several minutes, Janey found a column with a keypad and small screen, sunken into its surface. This must be the entry system to his Spylab, she thought. Yes!

There was a code to crack in order to gain entry but Janey was not concerned. Codes and puzzles were her particular strength. She looked at the letters, which blinked on the screen.

DYSYR UPIT SWAUEW

Janey looked at them again. The really didn't make any sense. She hesitated, her gloved fingers hanging over the keyboard that would allow her to enter if she could just crack the code.   What should she type? Her brain clicked into action, as she mentally scanned through possible solutions. And suddenly it came to her. Each of the letters in the three words was in a particular position on the keyboard. She looked to the left of D. *S*. To the right of Y was *T*. Then S again, so that would be A.   She continued until she had spelt on the coded message.

STATE YOUR DESIRE

Well, anyone at this column wanted to enter the Spylab so Janey carefully keyed in the word 'ENTER' using the same code as the one she had just cracked. 'W … B … R …W … E'

And to her joy and relief, the ground beneath her feet gave way. She had just enough time to whip round and wave to the stream of space-suited figures making their way from the rocket before she found herself sliding down a long tunnel.

The entry tube was obviously operated by some kind of air lock – and at the bottom there was a slight pause and a loud sucking noise before Janey – minus her spacesuit – was spat out into the Spylab.   The place was empty and Janey crept along the corridors, surprised to find that for once Copernicus's lab was not black. It was golden. Just like her new spysuit.

After a few minutes she came upon a vast bank of windows, very similar to the Launch Control Centre she had been in just hours ago. Janey peeped around the corner. There was Copernicus, pointing out various things on a screen before him to Twelve, who stared back at him with sad, dark eyes. Janey watched the boy shake his head, then drop his chin, then shake his head again, and she remembered again what G-Mamma had said about him at the beach. He couldn't speak. 'Of course!' she said. 'He's using sign language.'

She Zoomed in with her Ultra-gogs: Twelve was repeating the same sign again. At least, it was almost the same sign. He was doing two signs rapidly, over and over: two fingers from his right hand slapped against the palm of his left; the index finger of his right hand pointing to the fourth finger on his left. His head rattled from side to side. 'No,' she said, mimicking him. 'He's saying no.' And that must be what the signs meant. N and O. No. Two fingers on the palm – N. Fourth finger on the left hand – O.

But what was he saying 'no' to? Janey fished out her SPIPod and turned up the volume. Instantly she could hear what Copernicus was saying as he pointed to the huge screen in front of him, that showed outer space, with the Earth in the distance, and something like the point of an enormous pencil angled towards it.

'...the laser beam,' Copernicus was saying urgently. 'Just one press. We'll all be here. They'll all be there.'

N ...O ... signed the little boy, rattling his head back and forth.

'They won't feel anything!' Copernicus' voice was getting louder and higher. He was getting angry, Janey knew. 'The laser beam is painless.'

But Twelve was not to be convinced, and he started to back away from his father.

A tentacle seized him around the wrist. 'Oh, no you don't, boy. The first son gave up on me. I won't let you do it too.' And he flung Twelve backwards across the Control Centre floor.

Janey wanted to rush in and grab Twelve, but at that moment the two gorillas entered the room. Although ... when she looked again they seemed less like gorillas and more like *men*. So he did have some of his henchmen with him on the planet, and now they were picking up Twelve as if he were dropped litter, and carrying him out of the room.

Janey sprinted down the corridor as fast as her Four-Fs would allow. Finally she found herself at a lift, and slapping the button, she scrambled in and closed the door just as the henchmen were rounding the corner.

She got out at the next floor, and immediately heard her mother's voice. 'But it must be a dream. I've had a lot of them in the last year. Maybe it's time I saw someone ...' It sounded as though she was in the next room, but when Janey found it empty she remembered that she still had her SPIPod on. It took a few minutes and the search of at least ten rooms before she found her mother, sitting on the edge of a bed talking to Leaf.

'I wonder what the whole Squid thing means?' Jean Brown was saying. 'It's a recurring nightmare. Must mean something. Oh, Janey!'

131

Leaf spun around at the mention of her name, but Jean hardly seemed surprised that her daughter had just turned up in the middle of yet another strange hallucination.

'I have been telling your mother that this is all real,' said Leaf after he'd recovered himself. 'But she does not believe it.'

Janey ran over and gave her mum the most enormous hug imaginable. 'It is real, Mum,' she said. 'And I'm sick of lying to you, and pretending, and you being the only one who doesn't know what's going on. I'm going to tell you. Leaf, mind the door, would you?'

'Sure,' he said, making sure it was closed behind him and looking out through the little glass panel.

Janey's mum frowned. 'I'm really not sure you're—'

'I am real,' interrupted Janey. 'It's all true. And I'm going to tell you. Everything.'

Chapter 16 Hand signals

J ean Brown listened without interruption as her daughter described everything that had happened since G-Mamma first turned up at the gates of Winton High, and quite a few things that had happened before (including the fact that Jean Brown had once been Gina Bellarina, married to Superspy Boz Brilliance Brown.)

'And now it looks like Copernicus has built his own planet with some super-sized bit of the core of the earth, and he's planning on doing something terrible with a laser beam. Plus, he's been leaked the secret of R-Evolution, Dad's biggest discovery – oh and he has all these *apes* up here too. I don't know what for,' finished Janey eventually. She looked at her mother, who hadn't moved for the best part of an hour. 'So … what do you think?'

It was Leaf who first threw in a question, however. 'So Copernicus has really abandoned his own son and tried to kill him?'

'Really. Who would do that to their child?' Jean Brown's voice was barely more than a whisper.

'Mum, do you believe me?'

Jean stood up, wiping her hands down her trousers. 'Janey, what can I say? You tell me that for the best part of a year now you've been crawling in and out of the fireplace like a jack-in-a-box; that the dreadful Rosie Wotsits is your tutor or something …'

'SPI:KE,' said Janey and Leaf together.

'Well,, whatever you want to call it,' said Jean with a toss of her head. 'And the man I'm in business with is some reincarnation of your father who isn't dead after all. It's all nonsense. It has to be. I'm just caught up in one of those strange dreams again.'

'It is not a dream,' said Leaf. 'It is more like a nightmare, I suppose, but it is very real.'

Jean cast a wary eye in Leaf's direction, and then turned to Janey. 'Wake me up. Wake me up now, and I'll be able to forget all this.'

'But I don't want you to forget it all, Mum,' said Janey. 'I don't want to tell lies any more. And I don't want Dad to have to pretend to you either. If you know the truth, we can be a family again.'

At this Jean rolled her eyes towards the ceiling, but did a double-take as they slid past the glass pane in the door. 'Oh, here we go again. Squid man.'

With a gasp, Janey spun around. The panel was filled now by an evil yellow eye, taking in the three of them with a malevolent curiosity and more than a hint of hatred. The door slid open. 'Blonde. Again. You have a curious knack for being in the wrong place at the wrong time,' snapped the grotesque creature.

And before Janey could speak a tentacle had coiled around her waist, and another around her mother's, and they were yanked out into the corridor. Leaf staggered after them.

'You know, for a dream-monster, you actually hurt rather a lot,' barked Janey's mother, trying to struggle out of the tentacle's hold and grab Janey's hand at the same time. 'Put us down.'

At that, Copernicus simply dropped her And Jean collapsed on the floor 'Your wish is my command, Bellarina,' hissed Copernicus, a thin rasping sound grating from the back of his throat. 'And here's your darling spylet daughter.'

In one smooth move, he swiped his tentacle across a keypad at a nearby door, placed another tentacle on Jean Brown's back, and shoved her across the glossy, polished corridor-floor into the room he had just opened up. Janey was thrown in behind her, and just managed to forward-roll to the right so that she didn't collide with her mother. The door slammed behind them and darkness descended.

'What is going on?' said Jean, groping for Janey's hand in the gloom. 'Are you all right?'

But before Janey could answer, her mother let out a blood-curdling scream. 'Argh! We're in a dungeon. With rats! A rat just ran across my leg. I hate rats! Hate them! Oh, it squeaked. It's coming back …'

Janey reflected the laser of her Girl Gauntlet onto her golden suit and a warm amber glow radiated out across the room and a small creature ventured out of the darkness. Janey reached out an arm, and the creature ran up and sat on her shoulder. 'Look, it's a monkey. A really tiny one.'

Overcoming her horror, Jean Brown stared at it. 'I think it's a marmoset. A pygmy marmoset. We've seen them at the zoo.' She chucked it under the chin and the marmoset chattered obligingly. 'Aw. Poor little thing.'

But her words were drowned out by the sudden screeching and gibbering of a menagerie of monkeys, accompanied by some loud guttural bellows and an odd thumping sound belting out a bass-line. It was like listening to a very bad school orchestra tuning up.

'Don't move,' said Janey.

'I'm going nowhere,' replied her mother with a groan. 'Except the psychiatrist's when I wake up,' she added darkly.

Handing the squirrel-sized marmoset to her mother, Janey shuffled forward. She headed for the nearest sound – a quiet gibbering which sounded more desperate than threatening – and suddenly a cage came into view. Behind the bars was a chimpanzee ... no, several chimpanzees, their eyes wild and full of fear. 'It's okay,' said Janey softly. 'I won't hurt you.'

She did a quick headcount of the eleven chimps and moved on around the room. The next cage held a variety of smaller monkeys: lemurs, more marmosets, tiny tamarins with strange lion-like faces. The marmoset had obviously managed to slip between the wires of its cage.

'Janey, what are you doing? I can't see you.'

'I'm just finding out where we are and who's in here with us,' said Janey. Baboons and gibbons were in the next cage, glaring at her indignantly and then turning their back with disdain. 'The room is massive. And it's full of apes in cages. This one's got ... um, orangutans, I think. And that weird thumping sound came from the gorillas.'

Jean sighed. 'So we're trapped with a bunch of wild animals. Marvellous.'

'Someone's coming!' Smothering the light from her laser by curling her finger into her palm, Janey slithered back across the room and threw herself down next to her mother.

There was a scratching sound at the door, and Janey heard her mother's breath quicken as the door handle rattled. Yet the door stayed closed. Someone trying to get in – someone who didn't have the right codes or finger-prints to gain access. 'I bet it's the spy team!' she whispered. 'Night vision, and zoom.'

'Pardon?' said her mother.

Janey laughed. 'Not you. My glasses. Ultra-gogs. I need to see who's at the door, and if it's Alfie or the others we can ...'

But it wasn't one of her spy friends. It was a little boy, too small to see through the glass panel into the room from the floor. From the angle of the door handle and the peculiar sideways manner in which he was staring into the room, Janey guessed that he must be standing on the handle and hanging onto the top of the door frame. And judging by the way he moved his head back and forth, he was searching for something.

Janey felt sorry for him. He might be Copernicus' son, but so was Alfie, and it wasn't anything he was proud of. In fact, Twelve looked just about as reluctant to do his father's bidding as Alfie did. Her instincts told her that Twelve was not an enemy. She'd been wrong before, but this time Jane Blonde would have staked her life on the fact that Twelve was not on the side of evil.

'It's a little boy,' she told her mum, realising that Jean did not have the advantage of Ultra-Gogs. 'Remember the boy we saw on the beach.'

'Oh yes. The one in the rocket with us,' said Jean. She let out a brittle laugh. 'Listen to me. *The one on the rocket.* As if it were actually true!'

'He's looking for something. I'm going to help him.' Without giving herself the chance to think through it more logically, Janey pointed her laser finger at her Spysuit and pressed. The same ambient glow filtered out across the room, and the boy's head snapped round towards her. As soon as he'd registered who she was, his face fell, and he started to peer around the room again. 'Well, it's not us he's interested in,' said Janey. 'Come with me, Mum.'

Shuffling around in a close-linked pair, the marmoset still on Jean Brown's shoulder, Janey and her mother edged towards the gorilla cage. Once the two inhabitants were lit up, swaying restlessly on their enormous knuckles, Janey looked straight into the boy's eyes. He gazed at her for a moment, and then in a tiny shadow of a movement, he shook his head.

138

'Not the gorillas then.' Janey guided her mother across to the orangutans and glanced at Twelve. Again, he shook his head, glancing back along the corridor nervously before shaking his head at Janey, more emphatically this time. 'He can hear someone coming. Quickly.' They stumbled sideways and illuminated the mesh enclosure of the smaller monkeys. No. Tears were welling up in Twelve's eyes. Janey hurried on. There was only one cage left. The chimpanzees with their quiet, desperate chattering. One was clinging to the bars at the front of the cage, and her eyes – somehow Janey knew it was a girl, another girl, like herself – glimmered in the laser light with something that could have been tears too.

And when Janey saw the expression of joy that spread up Twelve's face at the sight of the chimpanzee, she knew that she had found what he was looking for. 'It's this one,' she said, and moved closer to the cage so that Twelve would have a better view.

Jean looked for a moment, then reached out a hand to the chimpanzee's fingers. 'Poor little thing. Is it his pet, do you think?'

'Must be. He's waving.'

He was also beginning to look very panicked, Janey noticed. He waved again, turned his head back along the corridor, and then turned to stare at Janey with such pleading in his eyes that Janey understood. These two – this boy and this chimp – wanted to be together. She knew it. When she recalled what he had drawn on the beach, she was absolutely sure. It wasn't potatoes. It wasn't food at all. It had been a clumsy attempt by a small boy to draw a chimpanzee.

But what could she do? She lifted her arms and hands, tilted her head to one side, and shrugged. *It's hopeless*, she was trying to say. *I don't know what to do. Tell me how to help. Why's this one so important?*

But of course, he could not speak. 'But he can speak sign language,' she said suddenly.

Quickly, she linked her pinky fingers together, tapped her fourth finger on her left hand twice, then slapped two fingers into her left palm. Then she nodded towards the chimpanzee, as if to say, 'Shall I tell her?'

And at that moment great tears started to roll down Twelve's face. He nodded, then shrugged helplessly, then whipped around to stare back down the corridor. What was it she had said? Janey knew that the two fingers and the fourth finger had spelled out, NO. It was the most urgent puzzle she had ever had to work out. 'N' was two fingers. O was a tap on the fourth finger. O was the fourth … something. But the fourth what?

And like a lightning strike, the knowledge hit Janey in the brain. O was the fourth vowel. The word he'd been spelling out ended with N, had two O's preceding it, and the first letter was something to do with two links, formed in this case by the two little fingers joined together. 'Moon,' she said hopefully. Twelve shook his head. 'Two links … I … I don't know … oh! S!' she cried. 'Soon!'

140

Twelve nodded furiously as Jean said, 'What?' Janey had no time to explain.

'Soon. You'll get her out soon?'

At that the boy's little face crumpled. He shook his head sadly, and Janey understood. It was too late. Janey's breath caught in her throat. The boy looked devastated. Carefully moving one hand off the door-frame, he held a fist near his heart in a gesture that Janey couldn't mistake. 'You love her. I'll tell her,' she shouted, hoping he could hear her through the thick door. 'I'll tell her you love her. Is she your pet?'

But now Twelve turned around again. Someone was coming. He dropped out of sight, but just as Janey was turning to pass on his message to the chimpanzee, she saw both of his small hands in the window. He needed two hands, but wasn't tall enough to see through at the same time so was reaching out above his head, his back to the door so Janey could see what he was saying.

Both pinkies linked together. S.

The index finger of the right hand tapping the middle finger of the left. No idea.

Both pinkies linked again. S.

A time-out sign?

The index finger of the right hand tapping the index finger of his left hand.

Finally, his right index finger crooked against his left palm.

Then the hands were whipped out of sight and footsteps rattled away down the corridor.

'Oh, I don't know what it means. S … something … S. SOS?' Janey spread her hands and wiggled her fingers in frustration. 'No, it can't be because O was the fourth finger. So the fingers are vowels, the middle finger would be … A … E … I. It's I. SIS…'

Janey stopped short, looking up at her mum who was watching her in complete bewilderment. 'S. I. S,' she whispered. 'Then a time-out sign. Or maybe that's the sign for 'T'. Second finger on the left hand, the second vowel. That's E. S …I…S…T…E…' And she put her rounded index finger in her palm as Twelve had done.

'R,' said Jean Brown, looking at the shape Janey had made. 'Definitely R. S.I.S.T.E.R. But what does that mean?'

'Sister.' Janey's voice could hardly get through her closed throat as she turned to look at the sad eyes of the chimpanzees. 'She's his sister.'

'But he's a boy,' said Jean.

But Janey knew the truth. 'He is now, but he wasn't always,' she said, the full horror of what she had just discovered nudging against her brain, a dark shadow, threatening, deathly. 'It's R-Evolution. Rapid Evolution. That's why Copernicus has got all these apes.'

She turned slowly to look at the faces behind the bars. There'd been more apes on the rocket.

It was monstrous. 'He's not Twelve's father. He hasn't even given him a name. Just a number. There were twelve chimpanzees, and he was the twelfth. Copernicus *made* him, Mum. And he's got all these other here so he can put them through the R-Evolution process.'

Janey swallowed as her mother stared at her, puzzled. 'You don't mean ...' said Jean, slowly working it out.

'He's changing all these apes. Into humans.' Janey could hardly believe it, but she knew that Copernicus was capable of anything. 'He's making his own human race.'

And as soon as the words were out of her mouth, Janey understood what he planned to do. He would have his own breed of humans, spies, Copernicus followers. So he would have no use for the other, existing human race. In fact, they would simply get in the way.

Jane Blonde, for one, intended to get in the way one last time. 'Gina Bellarina,' she said urgently. 'We have to get out of here.'

With a quick smile at the startled expression in her mother's eyes, Janey headed for the gorilla cage, just as someone else appeared at the door.

Chapter 17 Tube signs

As Janey released the gorillas from their cage, the door blasted open with G-Mamma, Mrs Halliday, Alfie and Tish still attached to it by the feet. The combined explosions of their Four-Fs had been enough to tear it from its hinges. Now the gorillas sprang into action, wrenching off the fronts of the cages, beating out a wild threatening tattoo on their enormous chests, as they followed the other escaping primates along the corridor.

'Great gorilla bums!' G-Mamma covered her face from the floor where she was still lying. 'Don't let that thing stand on me!'

Janey helped her up. 'They've gone. But there are others.'

'We know that, Blonde,' said Tish. 'Two of them – well, we thought they were gorillas but they turned out to be men – found us having a sneaky peek into Mission Control.'

'We were thrown in a great storage room with a load of them,' said Alfie with a look of disgust. 'The stench was disgusting.'

'Hmm. You've obviously never emptied your PE bag,' said his mother. 'Jean. Janey. Are you both okay?'

Jean shot her a dark look, just the hint of a question hovering at the edges. 'Apart from wishing we'd gone to Bournemouth on holiday, I think we're fine.'

But Janey knew they were going to be far from fine if they didn't act quickly. 'Listen: the little boy, Twelve, is an ex-chimpanzee. Those guards used to be gorillas. Copernicus is going to Revolutionise all those apes into humans, and then I bet he'll try and destroy Earth with that laser beam he's got trained on it.'

'And you know all this how?' said Alfie.

Janey knew it because it all made sense. The logic, warped as it was, worked perfectly. In changing hippos into killer whales, Copernicus had been trying out the Revolution process. Once he'd perfected it, he'd tried it on a chimp and managed to turn it successfully – although Janey wasn't really sure if it could count as 'success' – into a little boy. He knew he could do it, and now he was shipping apes away from Earth to populate a whole new planet. It was what he'd always wanted to do. Rule the universe. He'd even made his planet golden like the sun, just to be sure everything revolved around him: the Sun King.

'There's just something I want to check,' she said as she reached for her PERSPIRE. 'Let's see.' She typed SIGN LANGUAGE into the search engine and enough a diagram popped up showing that she'd guessed correctly. Twelve definitely had been saying 'Soon', 'No,' and, most disturbingly, 'Sister.'

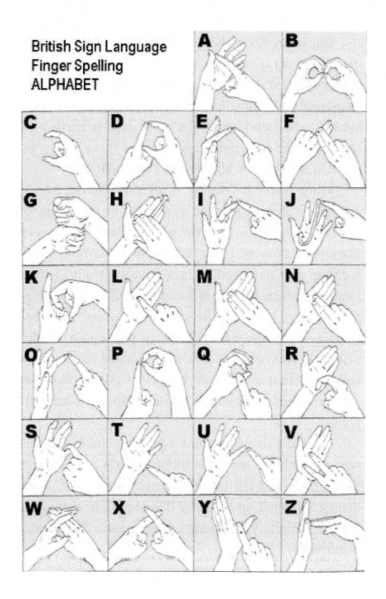

British Sign Language
Finger Spelling
ALPHABET

She showed the others. 'Far out,' whistled Alfie. 'So he *made* Twelve and now he's passing him off as his son. Hey.' A look of horror flashed across his face as a thought occurred to him. 'You don't think that I …'

'It would explain a lot, Monkey Boy,' said G-Mamma.

His mother snorted. 'Don't be silly, Alfie. You're perfectly normal. Ish.'

Janey spoke quickly and decisively. 'We've got to get the other apes away from here so that they can't be R-Evolutionized too.'

'Back to Earth?' said Tish hopefully.

'I'm not sure Earth's going to last very long,' said Janey quietly. 'Get as many as you can on the rocket. There may be another way out of here…' Copernicus had appeared out of nowhere when she saw him as she left the rocket. There had to be another way of coming and going from his planet. 'I'll go out and check.'

Janey ran on ahead, anxious to see what their other escape route might be. Although she knew that before they escaped she'd have to find out more about Copernicus's laser beam. There was no point going back to Earth if he still had the means to destroy it. Although how a laser beam could destroy it, she wasn't sure …

It was only as she shot up the entry tube that Janey realised she hadn't stopped to put on a space suit. Fear gripped her insides: without the space protection and the gravity boots, she might well find herself launched out of the tube and straight into space. There was no way she could stop and so Janey thrust her SPIder between her lips and chewed furiously. If it supplied oxygen under water without any hiccups, maybe it could do the same for her in space.

She popped out of the entry tube and looked around. The 'Copernicus' bus stop was just visible in the distance, and she strode towards it, leaping in strange clumsy bounds as her Four-Fs ripped away from the planet and then made contact again with an odd magnetic pull. The Super-sized piece of earth's core that stabilized the planet obviously gave it some form of gravity, but it was not quite like walking on Earth.

When she reached the bus stop she stopped and gave it a long, hard look. It wasn't a bus-stop, she suddenly realised. This was more like a sign on the subway. As she looked at it, she recalled what Copernicus had said back in Florida. Back on Earth. He said he'd be taking the *tube*. Could he really have meant it? Literally? Could this possibly be a ... tube station? The disk of weird, shimmering weird beside her seemed to whirl for a moment, like water disappearing down a plug-hole.

She couldn't risk trying it herself and there was only one thing she was carrying that she could afford to lose. She wriggled the signal mirror out of her pocket, and held it out towards the disk of wind. The little silver circle nosed into the wind, and two things happened at once. The wind suddenly sucked so hard that Janey could barely hold onto the mirror, and in the same moment four names flashed up under 'Copernicus' on the tube sign: Moon, Canaveral, Sunny Jim's, Antarctica.

The shock of seeing the other locations of Copernicus' Spylabs made her release her grip on the mirror. The wind immediately took firm hold of the little stick and whisked it away. Janey couldn't see where exactly, but by the way the word 'Canaveral' was flashing, she guessed that the Spylab under the Kennedy Space Center was where the mirror was headed. She was so busy staring at the sign that for several moments, Janey did not realise that the beeping sound in her ear was coming from one of her own spy-buys.

'At last,' she thought, tearing off her PERSPIRE. 'An email!.'

AT SPACE CENTER WITH BIRDS 'N' DIVAN. SUFFOCATING HEAT. WHERE DO WE FIND YOU? A X

Janey translated quickly. Her dad had got her SOS email, followed them to Florida with Eagle, Peregrine, Blackbird, Rook, and Ivan Erikssen – the Birds and Ivan. She needed to brief him on the whole situation before the sleeping sickness caused by the heat took hold of him. Ignoring the strange grinding sensation that was juddering through the ground, Janey typed out a message.

'FIND TUBE,' she wrote. 'THERE MUST BE …'

But she never got to finish. Dropping her PERSPIRE, she ducked as a laser beam shot over her head. She looked around. There was nobody else on the surface of the planet, but just beyond the entry tube to the Spylab a giant zapper was poking out of a hole. Pointing directly at her. She had two choices. She could leap down the Tube to another of Copernicus's labs, and more or less ensure her own safety. Or she could get back to the entry tube, back to the people she loved, and try to make some difference to their fight.

It was no choice at all, really.

Stuffing her PERSPIRE back on her head, Janey crawled on her elbows as far as she could, then stood up and tried to make a run for the entry tube. She galloped across the sandy surface, launching herself as high as she could to leap over a low-flying laser beam shot, bounding left and right like some crazed gazelle in an attempt to dodge the radiant shots of light that were aiming directly at her. She had the entry tube in sight. She reached out to punch in the code, the code she had worked out herself, and just as she was to jump away from the keypad, arm outstretched, her other arm out to balance herself, legs in a star jump, a perfect golden X-marks-the-spot, the laser beam caught her, full in the middle, and she tumbled, doubled over, into the top of the entry tube, as blackness closed in around her.

Chapter 18 Laser boy

With a start, she came to instantly as the entry tube suctioned her through its lower levels and then jettisoned her neatly into the Spylab corridor. Janey checked her stomach. There was a slight warm patch - the arrow of golden light had obviously touched her but it had not pierced her spysuit. In fact, she didn't feel too bad, apart from a slight need to shake her head and yawn.

The figures all around her had not fared so well, however. Piled up against the walls of the corridor, slumped wherever they had fallen, were mounds of monkeys, chimpanzees, orangutans, and gorillas.

'Oh no.' Janey spat out her SPIder and thrust it into a pocket of her golden suit as she looked around. She touched the nearest primates. It was Twelve's sister, she was sure of it. How was she going to tell him that his sister was dead? But then she felt the warmth beneath her fingers. They weren't dead. They were sedated. They had all been knocked out, and along with them were her spy friends.

What on earth – or on planet Copernicus – could have caused such carnage?

And then she saw it - laser firing from around the corner ahead of her, attached to a fat-handled gun like the super-soaker water pistols Alfie and Leaf had played with at the pool in Florida. Even more shockingly the zapper that was now firing at her was clasped firmly in a slender hand which poked from a green cuff edged with gold.

As Leaf fired again, Janey dodged the laser beam and it glanced off her side. But Alfie took the hit, and groaned loudly before passing out completely.

'Leaf!' cried Janey, outraged. 'What are you doing?'

His answer was to lunge back into the corridor and shoot a couple of yellow lasers at her again. She was hit in the shoulder, and then the hip, but other than a slight warmth and the need to yawn, Janey felt fine. Why were the others affected so badly when she wasn't?

Jane Blonde did not need to know the answer, however, to know that she had just discovered a huge advantage. Leaf's weapon couldn't hurt her. As soon as he appeared around the corner again, Janey banged her Four-Fs against the floor and leapt at him. In less than half a second she had flown across to him, taking the full impact of a dozen BLAM-BLAMs from the laser gun, yet not slowing at all. Before Leaf knew what had hit him, she had ripped the gun from his hands, drop-kicked him to the floor, and sat on his legs.

'You.' Janey could hardly bear to look at him. 'You're the double agent. You were the one passing the Revolution secrets to Copernicus.'

Staring from Janey to the laser gun she was now brandishing, Leaf gave a tiny nod.

'That's how Mum ended up here! You'd already keyed in the coordinates when I grabbed the control from you.'

'Guilty,' said Leaf, wincing as Janey squashed his knees.

'How did you get into Solfari Lands?'

Leaf swallowed, his Adam's apple bobbing up and down his pale, slender throat. 'SATISPI,' he said quietly, his eyes slightly watery as he looked up at the angry spylet on his chest. 'I opened a hatch in the grass next to the Spylab. Nobody saw me because of the green suit.'

'And that's why you were never quite there whenever we were captured or in danger.' Janey poked him in the chest with the syringe end of the gun. 'Copernicus has been protecting you.'

Again, that barely perceptible nod.

Janey felt sickened. Here was yet another person she had trusted – that her father had trusted, who had turned out to be a double-crossing fake. She could not imagine what it would take to persuade someone to give up on their friends like that. 'Why, Leaf? Why would you do that? Your father has been a colleague of my dad's for decades.'

At the mention of his father, Leaf squirmed and bucked angrily, and suddenly Janey tumbled to the floor. The laser gun skidded out of her hands across the floor; she watched it skitter away, not worried anyway whether Leaf managed to get hold of it. It didn't seem to affect her. But when she looked around she found that Leaf had found his feet again. He was towering over her, pale, ghost-like, with a rather large sword clasped in two hands held above his head, the tip pointing at her heart, ready to plunge right through her.

'My father was never strong enough to claim what is rightfully ours,' he spat. 'He would rather be your father's … employee.'

Janey stared up at the sword, trying to work out if she had time to roll away if Leaf brought it down. There were strange symbols etched into the silver, and suddenly Janey recognized it. It was a Viking sword. Leaf was getting back to his ancestral roots, it seemed.

He spoke again. 'But *I* shall not be enslaved to your father. I am a leader. Copernicus has promised me ....'

Even as he said it, Janey saw a glimmer of doubt flit across his eyes, and she remembered him questioning how Copernicus could abandon his son. If he could do that to his own flesh and blood, what exactly were his promises worth? But Leaf shook his head as if to clear his thoughts, and dropped the sword even closer to Janey's ribs.

'He promised you what?' said Janey, not daring to take her eyes of the steely point that was only centimetres away from her heart.

And Leaf laughed. 'What is rightfully mine. America.'

Now Janey was convinced that Leaf, like Ariel and so many others before him, especially Copernicus himself, had gone mad.

'What on earth do you mean?'

'That's exactly it, Blonde,' said Leaf, removing a hand from the sword to brush his fair hair from his eyes. The sword swung dangerously and Janey tried to suck in her stomach to avoid being skewered on it. 'Earth is going to be taken over by Copernicus very soon, and when that happens, I will get America to rule over. You see,' he said gently, as if to a small child, as he got a firm grip on the hilt of the Viking sword again, 'Christopher Columbus was not the first European to discover America. It was my ancestor, Leif Erikssen, who first landed on these shores. It is we Vikings who should have been the founders of the whole nation, and run the government, ruled the world.'

There was a wild light in his eyes as he imagined the glories that should have belong to his race. 'He tricked you, Leaf,' Janey said gently. 'Copernicus was just using you to get my father's secrets. He's not a man of his word. You'll end up stuck on this planet. You might get to be in charge of a couple of monkeys if you're lucky.'

Doubt flickered across Leaf's face once more, but he shook his head firmly. 'No. He had protected me. My suit …' and he shook his cuff so that Janey could see the golden lining slide down beneath the green outer layer … 'and the space suit, the place in the rocket – all this he has done to protect me.'

But Janey shook her head. 'No, Leaf. He was just protecting himself.'

'No …' hissed Leaf, his bottom lip starting to curl like a worm.

155

'It's true,' said Janey, hoping he would do something stupid as he became more emotional.

He did. 'No!' he roared, and he thrust his hands up high above his head, ready to split Jane Blonde down the middle. She only had a tiny amount of time, less than a second, to slither out of the way of the plunging blade, but he'd catch her, surely, if not in the heart then in a shoulder or an arm or a thigh … there was nowhere to go … no way to escape.

Knowing it was hopeless, Janey flipped onto her front, and at the very same moment she heard a familiar voice say, 'I'll take that, thank you, Leaf,' followed by a few muffled thumps and grunts and the clang of a Viking sword as it clattered to the floor.

She looked up to find Leaf bound and gagged. Someone was standing over him, the sword now pointing perilously at his throat.

'Janey,' said Jean Brown, nodding down at her daughter, 'if we're ever going to get out of here I think I'd better start believing you. In fact, I was never sure I trusted this one,' she said. 'I was trying to tell you when you found me here, and you asked him to mind the door.'

'Mum,' said Janey in disbelief. 'You saved me! And you're all right … and you fought off Leaf'

'Well, he's just a boy really, and I am a Superspy, darling,' said Jean Brown, looking down at her neat tee-shirt and trousers as if she still couldn't believe it. 'Apparently,' she added.

It was harder still for Janey to believe. She'd hoped beyond all hope that her mum could accept what she'd told her, but somehow she'd never been terribly convinced that her mother would accept the truth. 'What changed your mind?'

'Ah, well, yes,' said her mother. 'I got left behind down the corridors I was wandering around, trying to find you, and I went past this room with big windows, and Squid Man was inside, and there was a great big screen with a huge one of these just showing on it.' She nudged the laser gun with her toe. 'Anyway, as I was watching, the picture sort of zoomed in, and I realised we were looking at Florida, at that Space Centre place. And then it zoomed in even closer and there on the floor was … your father.'

Janey gasped. She'd seen her dad!

'And the funny thing was, when I saw him there on the floor, knocked out, surrounded by all these other people dressed in peculiar spy-type gear, my insides went all funny and I shouted out … well, I shouted 'Boz'. Rather loudly.'

Janey had never felt happier. Her mum believed her! She knew everything! 'Oh, Mum,' she said with a sob 'We can be a family again.'

Jean dropped the sword and crouched down. 'Not if we don't stop old Squid Man,' she whispered. 'He's up to something terrible, I know it.'

Janey knew it too. The end of the Earth. The beginning of a new regime. Copernicus ruling from Planet Copernicus.

'Mum, wake the others up. There's a weird disc of wind near a 'Copernicus' tube-stop just outside the entrance – I know it sounds crazy but jump in it, all of you, and get off at the Moon. There's another Spylab there.'

Her mother looked at her, opened her mouth to say something, then shrugged. 'Landing on the moon is really no more outrageous than anything else I've been through in the last few days. I'll make sure we've all got our space suits on.' 'And what will you do, Janey? I mean … Blonde?'

Janey didn't know whether to laugh or cry, but knew that there was no time for either.

'I'm going to save the Earth,' she said. And throwing her Superspy mum a kiss, she sprinted away down the corridor, to the centre of all problems.

Mission Control.

Copernicus.

Chapter 19 Laser beam

The foul and disfigured Copernicus stood at the centre of Mission Control. Janey groaned as she saw who was standing next to him. Twelve.

She turned on her SPIpod. 'I don't have the manpower to round up all those escaped gibbering animals,' lisped Copernicus to the little boy. 'But I still have my Spy-clone machine. If they all escape, I'll make clone copies of you, Twelve. I'd better warn you though,' he added as if he actually cared for the boy, ' that the master version doesn't fare very well. You'll get all used up. Very quickly.' The great shoulders of the monstrous creature jiggled up and down. He was Janey looked directly at the screen – and her stomach heaved.   It was her father, lying passed out on a floor somewhere. The image on the screen zoomed out and Janey could now see that her dad was lying next to the Bird spy-family and Leaf's father, Ivan Erikssen. Now the image zoomed out again and Janey she could see the whole of Cape Canaveral. Then the Florida coastline, and the entire east coast of America. And all the time the rocket-length tip of the giant laser beam pointed accusingly down at the Earth. She instructed her Ultra-gogs to zoom in and on the laser and she noticed for the first time that there was writing along the side of it. Next to an embossed sun were the words LAY-Z BEAM.

Laser beam. She knew that already. Why was he directing it at the earth? Would it actually kill?

Jane Blonde looked left and right. There was nobody around to stop her, but no obvious way into Mission Control either. Then it came to her. There was a very obvious way to end up enter Mission Control. After turning her SPIpod to 'mic' for microphone, she lifted her bare left hand and hammered on the glass.

Copernicus spun around. 'B-Blonde!'

He could barely stand to utter her name, so outraged was he at the sight of her standing there, leaning on the window frame, shouting out to the boy: 'Twelve, get away from him! Run!'

It went just as she had planned. Infuriated, Copernicus stumbled towards the glass and lashed out with one of his enormous, grime-encrusted tentacles. The sound of the glass shattering, magnified by Janey's SPIpod microphone, made Janey drop to her knees, grasping at her ears. In that moment, Copernicus struck, and the next thing she knew, Janey had been gripped around the middle by a pulsating tentacle and was whistling through the air, straight down into Mission Control.

She slammed into the floor with a bone-crunching smack. 'Watch them, then!' Copernicus was screaming hysterically. 'Watch them all lose the will to live! Everyone you've ever known, Blonde! Everyone you've ever loved! They're all down there, all sucking up to your ridiculous father and his do-gooding type, when they should be listening to me! Me! Well, now they will. Now they will have no choice. No voice of their own. Now they will have … NO WILL!'

His hideous limbs thrashed like some insane conductor as he pointed at the screen, and flung Janey from his grasp.., His shrieking filled her entire head so that it felt like it would explode. Eyes scrunched up against the pain, Janey ripped off her SPIpod and threw it to one side, and instantly the relief came. She could now hear that Twelve was sobbing gently, shuffling as far back as he could under a bench , while a python-like tentacle reached out for her. It grabbed her by the ankle, and Janey suddenly found herself hanging upside downfacing the screen.

'Rotate 180 degrees!' she yelled at her Ultra-Gogs, and at once she could see the screen properly. The image had shifted once more. No longer were they looking at the coast of America; now the whole of America lay before her, and then there was the whole Earth, tilted below them like the globe in her classroom. Her lovely, ordinary classroom, in lovely, ordinary Winton School. Red figures were illuminated in the right corner. 60. 59. 58.

The one-minute countdown was on.

'Twelve!' she screamed. 'Jump! Get up to the window, get out, and go to the tube station. Find the others. Go! Go!'

With a frantic and fearful glance at Janey's upside-down face, Twelve took his chance and leapt onto the workbench. He then flung himself, monkey-like, up to a

161

dangling light shade, and swung across to the shattered window. After a last glance in her direction, he was gone.

Pulling herself up as far as she could, Janey sank her teeth into the hideous tentacle that was holding her captive, and Copernicus threw her to one side and drew in his tentacle limb in the same movement.

'Nasty girl. Anyway. Thirty seconds,' he gloated. 'Ah, look.'

Staring over at the screen, Janey saw that the Lay-Z beam was pointed at the North Pole. The top of the world. She said the words 'Lay-Z beam' out loud. And immediately she understood what Copernicus was doing.

It wasn't a laser beam as such. It was a *lazy* beam. He'd been directing it at Florida for weeks. That was why everyone was falling asleep. Losing the will to do anything. That's what had been affecting her team, and everyone else who seemed so sleepy all the time. And now he was going to cover the earth with apathy and laziness and the complete loss of will to do anything to resist him.

A Lazy Beam. It was almost brilliant, thought Janey. Copernicus didn't actually have to kill anyone. They'd just all be too sleepy and forgetful to bother to live any more.

Twenty seconds showed on the screen, the tip of the Lay-Z beam starting to glow bright amber. The colour reminded Janey of something. Her suit.

And in the very instant that she recalled how the Lay-Z beam had never affected her, she climbed on the workbench, slammed her feet into them, powered out through the window and Four-F'd towards the entry tube. Copernicus just threw back his monstrosity of a head, laughing.

But Janey knew she had a tiny chance. With fifteen seconds to go, she could just save the world.

Chapter 20 A ray of light

It had to work.

Shooting up the entry tube, Janey pulled off one of her Four-Fs and roughly shoved her SPIder into her mouth. The front legs snaked out between her lips, clamping around her nose, as the other six legs anchored themselves over her gums and pumped oxygen down her throat, just as her head hit the surface and she was flung out on to the sandy surface of Planet Copernicus. There could only be a few seconds left. The whole of Planet Copernicus vibrated beneath her feet.

Janey looked around frantically and spotted the great, glowing amber orb, attached to the end of the Lay-Z Beam like the venom at the tip of a bee sting. She skidded towards it, and could just make out a tiny blue-and-white globe coming into view below her. There could only be a few seconds left. The whole of Planet Copernicus vibrated beneath her feet.

.The golden orb was pulsating. It was gathering strength. Janey suddenly had the impression of a giant drawing its breath, ready to snuff out an enormous candle. Only this time, she thought, the candle was the Earth.

Planet Copernicus shuddered and grinded beneath her as it prepared to launch its attack of sleeping sickness upon the world.

Hardly knowing what she was doing, but knowing that it was the world's only chance, Jane Blonde bent down, ripped off her remaining Four-F spy shoe, and thrust herself up and out, straight ahead into the atmosphere, floating free in just a golden Spysuit and a peaked PERSPIRE hat.

In outer space.

'I'm completely mad,' she thought.

The end of the LAY-Z BEAM was right below her. With a breast-stroke action, Janey pulled herself through space – now she knew she was mad. She was actually swimming through space. The golden beam, quivering with scorpion evil, was next to her ... above her ... pointing right at her.

She could see the Earth. Janey couldn't help drawing in a breath at the beauty of the world below her, a tiny bead of decoration on the soft quilt of the universe.

But then a sensation of immense pressure made her turn over, away from the planet she was trying to save, looking back at the planet she had just jumped off into space. The golden orb of light appeared before her, bright as the sun, and then suddenly it was streaming towards her. Closing her eyes, she wriggled slightly to the right, and waited for the impact.

The full power of the LAY-Z BEAM hit her directly in her stomach, enveloping her in a burning cloud of primrose yellow light. The pain was immense. It was like being swallowed alive by the sun ... heat – unbearable heat, and blinding, agonizing light that seemed to cut through to the back of her brain, severing it in two, splitting her head apart …

And suddenly Janey realised the sensation of movement was not just limited to her stomach. She was hurtling, free-falling through space, eyes closed against the awful brilliance of the LAY-Z BEAM that had seemed somehow to become part of her. The SPIder was slipping from her mouth … she couldn't breathe … couldn't see … couldn't survive …

She was dying. Spinning, flipping, sailing through the atmosphere, she held out a hand towards the ever-growing blue planet beneath her. Earth. She could see it. One last time …

Then there was a flash and a crushing sense of pressure. At that moment her feet whipped round over her head; she looked back through her knees, and there was Planet Copernicus, brighter and more golden than ever, shimmering in the haze of the treacherous LAY-Z BEAM blast, reflected directly off her golden Blonde- suit, straight back at the source of its evil. As she shielded her eyes from the glare there was a gathering of light, an explosion that zapped out a cloudburst of phosphorescence, and then a crescent of brilliance crowned Planet Copernicus like an eclipse. And then the golden planet faded to grey. The reign of Copernicus was over.

Then there was another flash, nearer this time. And something tiny and white. Something she couldn't quite believe she could be seeing. And then Jane Blonde's brain

166

and the golden light blurred into one, and she knew nothing more.

Chapter 21 Goldenspy

Janey woke up in a hospital bed, still convinced that she was dead, with a whole team of spies and spylets around her and Trouble curled up at the end of the bed.

Seeing Janey's eyes open, her SPI:KE threw herself onto the bed and crushed Janey to her bosom. 'She's ALIVE! She's SURVIVED! Oh, sizzling sunsets, I can't help myself - I'm rapping even when I don't know I'm doing it. But I'm just so HAPPEEEEEEE.' She plastered Janey's cheeks with sticky magenta kisses until someone had the presence of mind to pull her off.

'You're not dead then?' said Alfie in his flat voice. Janey could see by the way he was twisting his lips that he was trying not to smile.

'I'm not sure,' said Janey. She checked her limbs under the sheets. Apart from being in some very scratchy singed spandex, they seemed fine. 'Are you?'

'Du-uh.' Alfie held out his arms and spun around. 'Definitely not.'

'We're all alive and well, thanks to you, Blonde,' said Mrs Halliday, patting Janey on the hand.

Memories came back to her in a flood: her mum, finally believing her; her dad, LAY-Z BEAMed on the ground at Cape Canaveral; the apes, the spies, Twelve, heading off for the tube. 'Dad ...Mum' she croaked suddenly.

'We're here, sweetheart,' said her mother.

We? Did she really mean … *we?*

The others cleared a path so that her parents could reach her bedside. To her astonishment, her father had his arm around her mum's shoulders, and Jean Brown had a definite air of something … something *spyish* about her.

Jean pulled Janey up from the bed and squeezed her shoulders. 'I thought you were right behind. That Tube just sucked me off Planet Copernicus and deposited me at the Moon station in seconds. I thought you'd be following.'

'I had things to do,' said Janey. She looked at her father. 'Did you know about the Tubes?'

He sighed. 'There's been talk for many years of tubes in space that we could travel through. Wormholes. Gravitational corridors. Whatever you want to call them, they form a network of invisible tunnels. What I can't believe is that Copernicus learned to harness their power before anyone else did.' He leaned over and kissed her cheek, adding quietly, 'These NASA scientists are very keen to talk to you about it.'

'NASA? We're still at Cape Canaveral then?'

Tish leaned over Abe's shoulder. 'Blonde, you discovered an unknown planet. Oh, and destroyed it. Of course we're still at Cape Canaveral.'

'That's what woke us all up,' said her father with a grin. 'That, and Ronnie dropping Trouble on my stomach with his sabre claw out.'

Janey still didn't understand.

169

'I …'

It didn't seem possible, somehow, but she remembered the golden beam ricocheting back off her golden suit, the flash of light behind her … 'Did I blow it up? Is Copernicus dead?' And Leaf, she thought. It saddened her. Leaf had been duped by Copernicus, but he'd looked as though he might just be reaching the point of changing his mind about his allegiances …

'Titian's exaggerating,' said her mother. 'You didn't destroy it. You just put it to sleep. Come see.'

Like a traveling circus troupe, a dozen spies and spylets accompanied Janey as she levered herself off the bed and made her way gingerly along the corridor. They passed a couple of burly security guards – who looked nothing like gorillas, Janey was glad to see – and found themselves at the end of a corridor. Two doors faced each other, both with another security guard outside with NASA emblazoned on their uniform.

With a nod from her father, Janey opened the door to her right. On a starkly made-up bed lay a crumpled body, snoring rudely. Leaf's Spysuit lay on a chair nearby, and Janey picked up the tattered lycra with its layers of green and gold. 'That's what made me realise I should jump in front of the LAY-Z BEAM,' she said slowly. 'I hadn't been affected by the rays like everyone else, and Leaf said he was okay too because of his suit. It had to be the gold. There was that man at Disneyworld in the yellow shirt – he seemed protected too.'

170

'That's right. Copernicus must have worked out when you weren't being affected, and then Leaf went into overdrive to get you to do anything where you might get changed.'

'Volleyball! Swimming!' It made sense now.

Abe nodded. 'The scientists think that because he was wearing it when the beam blasted back at the planet, he might not sleep forever. He could wake up in a while.'

It was only then that Janey noticed the figure to the other side of Leaf's bed. Ivan stood up with his head bowed, and reached out to shake Janey's hand. 'I can only apologise for my son's behaviour, as I have done to your father a million times.'

'Two million and counting,' shouted G-Mamma from the back of the crowd.

'I will stay here with Leaf until he wakes up, and then we will consider out future.' Ivan shrugged pitifully. 'At least it is a future on this planet. Thanks to you, Blonde.' He raked his hands through his thinning hair and sat down again.

'There's something else to see,' said her father gently, and they all shuffled outside and out of the way so that Janey could get to the door of the ward opposite. 'This person was dressed in black, so he didn't have the Goldenspy protection. It's believed that he will sleep for a long time. Perhaps forever – if we're lucky.'

Janey pushed open the door. There was no bed in this room. Instead there was a specially-created tank, and

171

sealed upright inside was the drooped and sleeping figure of a strange half-squid, half-human figure, with one eye huge and yellow, and the other human eye closed tight shut. Despite being sound asleep, the expression of the bleak squid eye still managed to look shocked, outraged.

'That eye's golden,' said Janey quietly. 'It might wake up.'

'It's blind,' said her father. 'And we'll never let him out of our sight again.'

Janey closed the door. Suddenly she felt exhausted herself. 'How long was I asleep?'

'About a week,' said Mrs Halliday as they walked back towards Janey's room. 'You might have had the golden spysuit, but you still took the entire blast from the LAY-Z BEAM yourself.'

'But how did I...I was just floating around in space, and then I saw this flash and a little white...a little white...'

At exactly that moment she spotted again what she had seen in space. A small white hand. Waving to her. Beckoning. This time it was waving from the doorway of her own ward.

Jean Brown hugged her. 'It was Twelve. Although we've decided to call him Jamie. We can't go on calling him by a number for ever.'

'For ever?'

'It's too dangerous to try to D-Evolve him,' said her father softly. 'And I never want to use R-Evolution again,

172

so we can't change his sister for him. We're all the family he's got.'

'We're … adopting him?' Janey looked from her parents to the little boy with the dark solemn eyes, gazing at her from the bedroom door. 'What did he do?' she whispered.

'Well, it was hard to work out what he wanted,' said her mother. 'None of us know sign language. But he got me to grab his ankle, then he dangled out into space, and grabbed you as you went by. Brave boy.'

'True spy material,' agreed her father.

As the other spies fell silent, Janey walked over to Jamie. He raised his eyebrows, and Janey just knew, instinctively, what he was asking.

She nodded, a tear spilling over onto her cheek. 'Yes, I'm okay. Thanks to you.'

He gave a small smile, and then started tapping out sign language.

'Oh, you're too fast for me. I'll have to learn … hang on, is that your name? You're telling me you're called Jamie.'

With a huge beam, he nodded enthusiastically. Janey crouched down in front of him. 'Do you know my name?'

His rapid sign language contained at least an A, an N and an E. 'Janey. Yes, but not just that.'

And on her knees in front of him, she pointed at herself and then at the boy, and lifted up her hands.

Both pinkies linked together.

The index finger of the right hand tapping the middle finger of the left.

Both pinkies linked again.

A time-out sign.

The index finger of the right hand tapping the index finger of her left hand.

Finally, her right index finger crooked against her left palm.

'Sister,' she whispered.

Jamie's eyes became bright with tears, and he flung himself into Janey's arms. When she turned around to look at the others, Janey noticed that they weren't the only ones looking a little teary. Even Alfie was clearing his throat and trying to look very interested in a placard about the misuse of mobile phones in technical areas.

Janey grinned. She was the luckiest girl in the world.

And as if on cue, G-Mamma held up her hands and rotated slowly to gather attention..

'A little rap to celebrate,' she said. 'Alfie and Rook, do this: Dum dum - chich. Dum dum - chich.'

'Yeah right,' said Alfie.

'Al Halo …' warned G-Mamma.

With a scornful roll of his eyes, Alfie said in a monotone, 'Dum dum Chick. Dum dum Chick.'

'Great! Now Blackbird and Titian, you can go BADA in between the dum dum chiches.'

Tish and Blackbird looked at each other, shrugged, and joined in with huge grins on their faces. With the Dum

Dum Chich BADA, Dum Dum Chich BADA rhythm going on behind her, G-Mamma swayed hypnotically.

'The goldenspy, she did survive,
She stayed alive, now gimme high five;
The goldenspy is Blonde all through,
It's what she do, lemme hear ya OO OO;
Goldenspy! Taking out the yellow eye.
Goldenspy! Through the heavens she can fly.
Goldenspy! Brown and Blonde rolled up in one.
Goldenspy! And she only just begun…'

G-Mamma and her little backing group hopped away down the corridor, and Janey watched her leave with a huge smile on her face. She yawned. This had been the most exhausting holiday ever. Which reminded her of something …

'Am I ready to leave hospital yet, Mum?'

Her mother tilted her head suspiciously. 'It's much too soon for another mission, Jane Blonde.'

And Janey smiled back at her mum, taking in her parents and her new little brother in a golden glow all of her own. This was going to be a completely different kind of mission. A new adventure.

'Let's go home,' she said.

THE END

ABOUT THE AUTHOR

Jill Marshall is a proud mum, nana and communications consultant, as well as the author of dozens of books for children, young adults and (old) adults. When she's not doing any of those things, she loves singing, dancing and theatre and going to see other people do singing, dancing and theatre. She divides her time between the UK and New Zealand, and hopes one day to travel between the two by SatiSPI.

Read the whole Jane Blonde series:
Jane Blonde Sensational Spylet
Jane Blonde Spies Trouble
Jane Blonde Twice the Spylet
Jane Blonde Spylet on Ice
Jane Blonde Goldenspy
Jane Blonde Spy in the Sky
Jane Blonde Spylets are Forever

Also featuring Jane Blonde–

S*W*A*G*G 1, Spook

OUT NOW!

Want the full SWAGG experience?

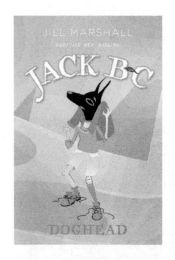

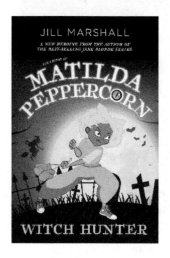

Immerse yourself in the origin stories.

The Jane Blonde series
Jane Blonde, Sensational Spylet
Jane Blonde Spies Trouble
Jane Blonde, Twice the Spylet
Jane Blonde, Spylet on Ice
Jane Blonde, Goldenspy
Jane Blonde, Spy in the Sky
Jane Blonde, Spylets are Forever

Jack BC in the Doghead trilogy
1 Jack BC, Doghead
2. Jack BC, Dogfight
3. Jack BC, Dogstar

The Legend of Matilda Peppercorn
TLOMP, Witch Hunter
TLOMP, Toadstone
TLOMP, Questioner
TLOMP, Trinity

Stein & Frank: Battle of the Undead People-Eaters

Also by Jill Marshall
Available in print, mobi, epub and audio.

For Young Adults
Pineapple
Fanmail
Lena's Fortune

For Adults
The Most Beautiful Man in the World
The Two Miss Parsons
As It Is on Telly

For younger children
Kave-Tina Rox

For more adventures and
information,

visit www.jillmarshallbooks.com

Follow Jill Marshall Books
on Facebook

Email jill on
info@jillmarshallbooks.com

Printed in Great Britain
by Amazon

38180657R00108